B S BHAMRA

TRIP SWITCH

SPIRIT FIVE

Published in 2020 by FeedARead.com Publishing

A CIP catalogue record for this title is available from the British Library.

INTRODUCTION

Benjmain and lucy are back on the planet earth and they are looking for trouble after numerous of number of attacks on the earth Benjmain is there to bring order and peace. With the ups and downs of the robot and lucy with the two sunflowers for company benjmain is being put through his paces.
Benjmains and lucy s relationship is nearing a end Lucy says she has had enough and her new attitude says it all as lucy has to watch her planet being watched by the spirit five and seems to think that she was going to be ordered to destroy it by the council in the city of Lou.

Benjmain has to correct her as they go on. The silhouette has made a move with the two cyber police men following it was a time of adventure an excited tie for benjmain.

PREFACE

In this particular story benjmain and lucy are against themselves and it works fine as the hitman and the oxygen ate two slowly disagreeing on the ideas of why benjmain had come all the way from his home town via a badge to protect what is left of what the planet earth was left.
With the ups and downs of benjamins and Lucy's relationship after a long battle through there minds in hope that they had come to an answer of what they could do to save the planet before it destroys itself. Would benjmain find an answers or would lucy sit back and watch her family as in the earthlings as she was one of them let them destroy it. They all said in the spirit five that it ws a beautiful place. It would be a shame to destroy it.

Lucy and benjamins have to make a discussion it was not going to be easy, as they both have there doubts. With some guidance form his friends benjmain still has not made an answer.

CHAPTER ONE

Benjmain ws busy going out of his mind the usual stuff, cold sweats headache visions that meant nothing at that moment, lucy was out of town benjmain ws on his own. Benjmain knows he is in trouble as he looks around for his fix to bring him right back, as benjmain tries to settle down and just as he speaks wishing that lucy was on board lucy appears walking in there's a smile on her face.

It was funny that his condition only seemed to have an effect him when he is at his most vunable time.
With everything around him his surroundings more normal it ws his condition and he did not understand himself fully when he felt like the way he felt. Only that he would have to rely on a badge and a space suit. Which both of them were glued together.

Benjmain close s his eyes for the first time controlling his feelings that were controlling him. Benjmain is still recovering after a good hour of Tormenting he has not told lucy yet that she has his condition all to come. He knows the badge as he wears it of course. It could be bad or even it could be good. And right now it was being bad hence the way that benjmain was behaving.

Benjamin needed a break he closes his eyes but not before climbing up o0n to his bunk on to his space bed. Benjmain was acting very out of character he ws alone and cold.
With Benjamins eyes closed he is talking to himself as well as lucy. Hoping that he finds somebody mostly lucy to answer his plea for normality once again.

Benjmain manages to talk himself back to sleep. However it was not long before his robot was by lucy side sending him a call through his mind benjmain still in his bunk receiving all kind s of images closes his eyes and chooses to ignore it. It ws not to long before lucy and the robot get worried about where benjmain was and how his condition was playing him.

Lucy tries to contact benjmain through her badge she gets no answer and neither does the robot the robot is thinking the worst. While lucy in a mood ws thinking why benjmain ws not answering his badge.
While benjamins ,lays on his bunk half unconscious he is dreaming of planet earth. As benjmain slips in and out of the dangerous dream. He sees lucy and then he sees the robot and he see s the robot and lucy and then he sees nothing they were all at the end oof a road in a normal street in a normal area not built up like most of the city they were all in a village, benjmain finds a small wood at the bottom of a street and it was there where he saw the images of himself.

Benjmain vison ws more than good and he could clearly see that he ws watching himself. He could see his family all around him.

Benjamin suddenly awakes he is all the way back in to the space ship he is in the spirit five. As he awake lucy and the robot are hailing him. As he ignores the bleeping sound of his uniform as he wakes he is taking his time. He already knew who ws on the other end of the call.

Benjamin smoothly turns on the intercom speaking loudly so he could be heard and so he could hear as he moved around the space ship floating touching buttons and repairing things. The things that he should of done before he had fallen asleep. The conversation starts.

Hay lucy benjmain your captain speaking is here how are you. What's going on down stairs on the planet earth. Lucy's first time reply ws a good one things are looking good down thee no troubles everything is like a rose flower. Benjmain butts in and he continues is my metal head friend my robot I hope that he has been behaving.

Lucy answers him. Er yes he's cool he's ready to come aboard he s got some samples for you we are ready to return to the spirit five. Do you read.
Benjamin continues this time he is butting in for the first time he ws excited, ok he says he would be there soon. Make sure that the robot is charged up he has some more duty's lucy reply was a good one a cool one. And continued that she would see him soon. Benjamin pushes a button the conversation comes to the end.

Only to restart again as benjmain had forgotten about there coordinates there's a creepy sound which ws quickly answered with a hay.
Hay lucy it is benjmain can you give me your coordinates please.

Lucy give s Benjamin there coordinates again and this time they get to the end of the conversation right they both hang up at the exactly the same time as benjmain had just told her that he ws on his way.

Benjmain ws getting used to the earth that he ws actually started to enjoy himself and it as before he had really disliked the planet earth and the earth people that went with the job. And with that the people that dwelled upon it.
As he changed so did benjamins attitude to the people to the people as they called themselves humans.
Benjmain wanted to meet them he wanted to make peace like they were surprised too. However with all the earths problems on the planet earth at this time it

would be very unlikely. Part of benjamins job was to make sure that the planet was destroyed.

Both lucy and benjmain ha discussed the thought over and both of them did not find a suitable answer. They still argue about it today.

Even though benjmain worked with closely with lucy who her self was an actual human he still believed that his job was the tougher one. Lucy did not believe benjmain. She believed that both being human which they were not as there counter part name was one of the same. Lucy had got that conversation right up side down it was the first time that she had totally cocked her conversations.

Benjmain controls the landing of there space ship smoothly a little different than Lucy's style of space ship landing. Lucy is first to board as she asks permission to step up aboard lucy once abord takes control of the space ship giving Benjamin a chance to breath. As she does her business the robot boards just after her.

Everyone is a board lucy takes control of the space ship as they leave again they discuss how they had landed in one piece.
Benjmain is still playing catch up with the robot a thought well programmed still actually needed the robot never the less benjmain stills plays with him asking him questions after question and receiving what benjmain liked some seriously intellectual answers.

The robot as benjamins liked the planet earth, and he said a lot to benjmain about the planet. It would be a shame if the human race would really destroy it. His words were some where along the lines of that it is a great place to learn it would be a great shame.

Benjmains ws surprised with the feelings that the ron=bot had and its honesty about the way he feels for the humans and the planet.
Benjmain was surprised with what the robot had said he tells him to tell lucy exactly what the robot had said to him. He repeats what he had said to benjmain and lucy who ws just as surprised as benjmain is.
Benjmain shouts to lucy that the robot ws growing feeling s and tells Lucy again loudly its not just him self and lucy but the sunflowers they to ha drown feelings to the robot so the robot ws not the only one. As for Lucy and benjmain they were friends and partners nothing more.

The robot questions benjmain s last comments about the words that he ws using benjmain is asked to explain what the word feelings was and meant the robot did not understand and benjmain was left to do the explaining. Meantime lucy was busy giggling as Benjamin has to give the robot a one to one.

Benjamin continued to the robot about the question to him about how he enjoyed the beech with the robot telling him that it felt soft and the butterfly on the sand dunes were good to talk to.
Benjmains tells lucy and lucy is smiling telling Benjamin that he had heard what ws said, just before as she shouts over to the robot to show benjmain the photographs as the robot tells Benjamin to take a look at what he had done. Look at the picture s the robot says.

Benjmain was looking as the robot tells him which ones were his fraviorte ones which was the one with lucy in it with himself next to her both holding small creatures from the ocean waters.

That's great Benjamin says I like that one and that one oh that nice benjmain continued. The robot had brought a lot of laughter in to benjamins and Lucy's heart in to benjamins space ship and the crew. They all siled a little more as the robot gives benjmain another picture of lucy surrounded by butterfly's.

As the robot with a little bit of help from lucy started to boast about things until all of them had enough about hearing from themselves. Once they had all settled down again for that evening until lucy decodes to stay up stating to benjmain who wanted to know why that she was not feeling tired and decided to watch the planet Earth from way up in the clouds not quite yet in to the atmosphere but close enough but well hidden away from any danger.

While lucy is watching the planet earth benjmain is listening to the radio broadcasts of anything and everything and anything that would be flying nearby them. Even so they could be invisible benjmain was still being cautious.
As benjmain has continued to worry as they had some close calls as for larger airplanes flying close to the spirit five leaves concerns to benjmain the planes signals could easily be jammed by the powers of the spirits fives systems. Benjmain did not want to cause any unnecessary accidents.

The spirit five had the same problem s under the ocean as for large tankers and other large ships could cause them the same problems.
Especially smaller crafts, It was not in benjamins job or protocol There was at least several distress call a night it ws not benjamins job to save these people it was the opposite.

This part of the job and it was benjamins job really had up set lucy. Lucy one not to complain ws botterling it all up in side of her and it was only on the occasional occasion that he would lose control, like now.

What's going on benjmain, he knew what ws going to happen simply by lucy s approach and her words what's going on. She only said those words when she ws angry.

Benjmain thinking quickly asks he to sit down close to him. What chair lucy continued. Just sit down and be quiet. Lucy repeats benjamins words back to herself quietly as she takes a seat. She ws being sarcastic lucy continues do not tell me because I do not know because you do not know there are real people down there.

Benjmain says nothing as lucy anger over what he had said was slowly boiling up over the edge lucy seemed to harden her voice setting louder and her words were more slurred. Why lucy says, benjmain shows no remorse over the conversation and lucy wants to question the whole thing again. As benjmain has no emotions.

Benjmain could feel her in the suit she was getting powerful with out the suit she ws as flimsy as any other human.

Benjmain could of suited her down which ws removing the suit from her was one way the others was to inject her with a serum made for her personally by the doctors team back on the planet of lou in the city.
At that point benjmain could not make up his mind the decision and he calls upon the robot to make the decision for him. They both decide to inject her with the serum she would sleep for day or two depending on how long her mood was she would wake up feeling more like her self. There were no side effects.

The robot and benjmain were now busy talking about some of the thoughts that lucy was shaving or could have been having. As they both come to the same concluding that she needed a break form everything. Even though she had just had one with the robot.
The robot continued if it was a wise decision as she had just got back with him and what had happened as a result form it.

What really happened down there robot the most they did was to play in the sea and stroll along the beach. The robot continued as benjmain is asking more questions she seemed happy enough to go into the ocean and she ahd said a few hellos to some passer by. Is that all benjmain qy she had lost control. benjmain asks not forgetting the real reasons why he ws questioning the robot and Benjmains thinks that lucy might of caught some thing and might of brought some thing on to the ship. That's could be the reason that she was acting out of character.

Benjmain wanted to know the real reason why she had lost her temper, while benjmain mind is into places as he know is thinking that maybe he might save her people except she still does not understand that it was not part of his job.

That part ws for lucy it would be left for her. Lucy did not play hard enough and her people would die. Benjamin with the robot continued the conversation benjmain ws asking all the questions and his robot ws giving him some serious answers. Of why lucy was acting like she was. As there conversation comes to the end lucy awakes with a smile on her face and some shouting she was back to normal.

CHAPTER TWO

Standing with an apology lucy breaks the ice again it was like it had never had happened benjmain was not going to start a conversation about what they interviewed and intended they both would rather wait for the whole incidents to reoccur again.

Benjmain has no feeling for the human race he made that clear to lucy and lucy was still was still trying to convince him tht her feeling cam from her heart the feeling s that she was having were her real feeling her love for the planet the feeling of love. Benjmain did not understand and when she tried to explain it would just go over his head he really did not understand.

It was all going over benjmain heathen re questions him.

Benjmain was convinced that it did not exist those word love. Lucy on the other hand ws convinced that it was his suit that was talking and not him. Not his mind that does the talking for Benjamin when lucy questions him. Benjmain has no answers and he has to answer her questions there was no way out. Benjmain and lucy are thinking about the word benjmain had been flawed he did not recognise the feeling the feeling s of love from one person to another person.

It was simple to the both of them that benjamins spirit five badge was in the way and it refused them both it did not understand the meaning of love of god.

It was a good question benjmain says I'll I will bring it up with council next time we are on there planet.

Benjmain takes full control of the sprit five, with the robot next to him by his side leaving lucy back at the back of the space ship doing the repairs. She was clearly still up set. And benjmain ws being ho9nest he did not know how to help her she was human. It was now her own problem and by the spirit five she ws going to have to figure it out all by her self. She would come back to benjmain once she was ready benjmain knew this could happen and he had explained to his council on his planet. There ws an apology to be made.

However lucy agreed that it ws not necessary. Lucy as benjmain was surprised and continued that thought it ws by her look on her face. Benjmain and the robot laugh it off and lucy smiled thinking tat it was funny then she catches on the robot and benjmain were having a laugh with her.

Of course sticking by the rule book.
Lucy reply was one of shock as she explains that she had spent a whole seven months reading the space book of its rule and regulations it was all made up. And none of the actual stuff exists. It was total rubbish.

Lucy with the book in one hand like welding a sandwich try's to rip it up failing miserable y and trys again not being able to remove the book only to put it back down on the dashboard of the spirit five only for Benjamin and the robot to laugh.

Lucy says to the both of them half smiling tht she would get her own back. Stating that there would be no more talking at bed time for at least a week then she changes her mind telling benjmain tat it could be a month the robot smiles as he disappears quickly he was taking her seriously and with that her reaction only for benjamins smile only for lucy to wipe the smiles of his face by telling him something similar.

Lucy agrees as much as benjmain that she needed an actual break from being in actual space benjmain gives her two choses the first was that she could go home and spend some time by her self on her own planet or she could continue in space full filling her duty and missions or she could go back to the city of Lou benjamins home planet.

Benjmain looks hard at the robot. The robot gives benjmain the ok and it ws done lucy ws going home but not before the council for there actual permission. Starting Infront of council of Lou was a scary place to be. And it took a lot of strength to do what lucy was going to do or even attempt not many people had tried. With the council guard the silhouette awaiting an argument and lucy coming out of her own mind asking for a break some time off.

It was all benjamins idea he thinks that lucy needed a break. Lucy could not pass the buck and was on her own. The council did not guess this as lucy awaits her answers. Benjmain is close by.

Lucy stands on trail as she trails her self with benjmain close by her side lucy is granted permission she has one month to clean up her act her self.

Benjmain is pulled aside and is collared for i9mbaressing the council once again Infront of a human being lucy. The silhouette was close by itching for an excuse to challenge benjmain once more. He ws close enough to benjmain to force him to make some informal spoken mistakes making benjmain approach a weak one.

As benjmain has to explain that he did not come all te way back to start trouble and he continued that he was there to help his partner. And that s why he ws there. He reminds them as he leaves with lucy out of the council rooms that he bears there badge and it clearly states spirit five upon it.

Telling g the council that the silhouette does not been badge because he is unworthy and neither did they which was an understate met because they all wore the same badge and with tht benjmain ws realising what he had said he had made himself look stupid.

As benjmain says this they all look at there badges trying to figure out what benjmain was talking about.

Benjmain on that account ws set free. Lucy is by his side as they walk out of the council rooms.
There was a several hour wait before the spirit five ws cleared for take off.
Benjmain and the robot took the time to finish the repairs on the spirit five a few hours more as they check

out the spirit five for any kind of danger and devices that may have been planted on the ship while they were away.

There would always be something and benjamins flowers would always tell him whom had been abroad while he ws on the planet earth doing his business nobody actually knew what there presents ws for although the robots was there mates the ships mates. They were the robots companions.

For once in benjamins life his paranoia had set its self a side, he was on board waiting lucy and the robots arrival as they moved both of them being checked out by the guards for clearance. Basically air port police. As lucy try's to explain and the guards miss understanding lucy until benjmain has to intervene.

Once all clear after being told by Benjamin to let her go ad pass with the robot they are all aboard and on there way back home to lucy home the planet earth. Just to drop lucy at home.

Lucy was going to start re living some of her old memories once again she was feeling nervous benjmain tells her it would be a close thing and that she should keep hold of the spirit five badge in case of any trouble they both agree. Within a few hours four to be precise in there minds they were back on the planet earth lucy has two weeks.

Lucy get off the space ship cargo side same old re enter they both laugh at lucy approach as in controlling there landing. As they continue to talk about being on the planet before giving it a good slagging off like they did not care but they did.
Enjoying your stay lucy Benjmains said as lucy is quick to reply that she needed the break. Benjmain tells her tat he would be close and with in that' second he had disappeared using his badge only to reappeared before he actually disappears completely.

Benjmains plan ws to use lucy as bate he had not told her about his pans the idea. Benjmain did not kwon the target and he ahd not told her about the deal that he ws making.
All benjmain knew and ws told was to keep close to lucy as she would be the target and within tat the thought had becomes benjamins.
Benjmain having trouble holding his tongue as he wanted to tell lucy it would no be long before she would notice benjmain was having to move fast faster than he liked.
He knew if he ws caught lucy would have a very long word with him and the spirit five. And after wards if it was to all go to the robots plan one thing for sure was that it was very really that the robot got things wrong.

Benjmain trusted the robots diessins more than his own which served in a sense that it ws right the second decision was his benjamins and so on as the third was Lucy's. Other than that they all trusted each other by word of mouth which was in fact law. With the space badge to support them they were a space team they were spirit five.

Lucy wants tom take a look around it was normal to explore even though she had her team there with her. However lucy did not trust anybody and even benjmain has to push her to convince her at the most of times. ,lucy ws no fool yet unbroken as she shuts the doors behind her as she was wishing that she had kept it open. As lucy was in such a rush to go and socialise nearly forgetting her keys to which she had left in the place that she had left them by her empty bottle of beer. As she picks up her keys it ws a little different from speaking to a built in to the robotic system where you could just say open ted or it was totally a different experience.

As she leave s the room for s second time as for being called back by her consciousness. This time leaving it. With the door unlocked thinking correctly having to turn around go back and lock it again. Finally afterward Lucy is on her way safely.

The robot gets a fix on the badge that lucy is wearing she gets in control of it as much as the robot does. Lucy does not no and is unconcerned that all eyes are on her. And both the robot and Benjamin are frilled lucy ahs frilled them both. It was lie she ws totally different when on her own and on the planet earth.

As lucy continued to introducing her self and socialising at the bar, the robot and benjmain are talking about what they were actually doing and they are now thinking that it ws a mistake and they should tell Lucy what they were doing using her as bate.

As they both watch in intersegment and all guilty but excited as it was not that bad of a plan. It was just awkward that they were using there team which ws a good thing but a dangerous one they both think that they could of been a little bit more honest to lucy. And both of them knowing that in the end that they would have to tell Lucy the truth in the end. Also thinking about the target. The robot reminds benjmain why he ws there to watch her and to stick to the plan and tells again why they were watching her at the hotel in the first place. Everything seemed to be on track she was defiantly a magnet for the rich men. Especially men in suits.

Lucy knew this and she knew that she could pull anybody she did not have to be told. She had a good body and kept herself well I suppose you could call her fit.
The robot and Benjamin and did not expect her to pull him or for him to pull her on the first night it ws moving slowly and this time benjmain had got in there early hoping that the target would get there . appear there early. Before the authorities would be about them. There ws always some body doing some thing and there ws always somebody taking making up stories it would only take one person a human to notice and once the word was out on the street and the cyber police would get on to the scene and itwould be game over for all of them.

Benjmain s and Lucy's plans and the robots plans would be rushed and un timed it was all the way back to the drawing board for the spirit five team.
The robot tell benjmain to relax and that they would have many chances ahead of them. Benjmain was little to be convinced. However he does what the robot asked.

As benjmain turns around pressing a few buttons on the space ships dashboard. As benjmain tinted the spirit fives main screen swinging a round backwards returning to his normal position pressing a few more buttons raising the space ship upwards and rising the main visor to protect them form the darkness of the planet then once again spinning around cloaking the space ship as he moves in to the position spinning back wards back in to another position his first position.

As he presses a few more buttons adjusting his seat for the second time not forgetting who un adjusted it as it ws lucy who never corrected his seat after using it. Benjmain would spend the whole night and early morning there.
benjmain wakes by the orbit and by his robot in the early hours of the morning the robot tells benjmain that lucy had gone benjmain jumps waking quickly where he says, the robot tells benjmain that she had gone of to the shops benjmain smiles and continues I thought you said gone as in taken a ride. They both smile no the robot adds just to the shops.
Benjmain corrects the robot benjmain knew that she ws in a safe place she had just gone to collect her morning papers.
Benjmain looking at the robot with sigh of relief the robot continues in have a fix on her she is close just a couple of streets away. I have a visual.

Benjmain smiles again leaning back wards in to a more comfortable position in his space chair.
With his hands behind his head.
Lucy is quick to return benjmain notices that on camera she looked different she moves differently.
They both agree that lucy ws acting differently un recognisable she gad changed when the robot sees this with the images and he agrees and then after a brief conversation agree that she had changed benjmain thinks that it ws only other humans that makes lucy think and cat the same as them.

Lucy ws disconcerted about things at that moment was enjoying her self benjmain notices tat she was different outside if te spirit five especially her space suit. She looked there ws a pause between them. Different the robot says. Benjmain agrees pointing at the camera.

It looked like lucy ws going shopping as she was hanging around a few streets down form her hotel and had popped in to a few shops. The robot speaking to benjmain asks him to come to the dashboard to watch the camera to watch lucy again.

Benjmain wanted to know how much money the robot gave her the robot looking confused and with a smile. The robot answers benjmain I left her your bank card and a ruck sack. Which colour card did you give her. The robot said the gold one.
Benjmain putting both hands on his head yelling softly that she was going to bleed that account dry. She ws a girl it ws shat they do.
The robot did not understand.
Benjmain jumps saying to himself repeatedly the gold one,
The robot answer's him again yes the gold one.
Ok think you would think that a girl with that kind of structure would come to he senses. As benjmain comes to the end of his conversations with the robot they both agree that lucy ws going to and had fallen in to a little bit of trouble paying for her ne bits.

As benjamins asks the robot to give him a close up of lucy using the bank card. Benjmains had just stopped sweating as he could now see the bank card that she ws

using. The robot had got it wrong and lucy had the right card which ws to run out of credit very soon. The argument ws not over benjmain ws angry as so was the robot. Benjmain continued so you thought you gave her the gold card however according to the computer you have given her my silver card good I can stop worrying. And so can you. The robot clearly did not understand. It did not understand the word money. Next time Benjmains still sounding like he ws in an argument tells the robot that in the future he would pack Lucy's ruck sack. They both agreed. The robot says nothing. Meantime lucy was off on a field trip. The robot insists that it ws not his fault and it was the spirit fives computers systems. It simply said that it was the gold card when the robot had asked.
Benjmain tells the robot that he ws really trying to understand continuing in a cocky mood that he really is trying to understand. Ok benjmain says its nots the ,money that I was worried about it was how many people noticed her. Because I can guarantee that lucy will blow our cover.

And do some ghastly act at the hotels table that's all.

That's all the robots says after benjmain.
Well you gave her the card ok I suppose that you were f]giving her some time off to have some fun. Then fact was when she gets to the casino we will let her play for a while if or as she starts to lose and she will I will or you will close her account through the space ships computer. Make sure this time that the card payments do not go through. Ok. Game over
If she tries to us it again the card in a few days we will activate it again if she goes to spend it again we will do the same again.

Agreed.
Agreed.

Benjmain ws feeling unhappy but was contempt with the idea of what they both had done. They look at her again. I am not feeling sorry Benjamin had to add. The robot says a little bit. There s nothing wrong with a little bit of fun.

Lucy had brought her self a few new belonging s and a few beers to se the evening off. the dress that she had brought her self on the gold card the dress was right and she looked good in it it was a little different than a space suit. As for the beer well that ws her own idea at that time.

Benjmain did not relaze that lucy ws a bit cute and both benjamin were a subject to talk about now when lucy ws not at home. Benjmain and the robot laugh as lucy

At Lucy's new look and at the same time gets a few looks from passers by she gets the look of who is running the town. As now lucy looked again once like lucy.
As the robots points out a figure which seemed to to appear in some of the robots video stats. Benjmain wants a clearer look so he goes the robot to get some clearer nearer shots. The robots eyes were good and he was congratulated when he spots what benjmain was worried about which to the point why they were there following her the first reason.
The robot had found the con man. And as he continued he grasped at the thought tat he thought that they were ten a penny in this town. The man that ws following lucy could have been employed by anybody. However when the computer pulls his profile there are pictures of thos man pulling wallets out of jackets and purses out of hang bags.

Benjmain need to get a message to lucy and the pick pocket ws left unspoken about until benjmain has more time as he tells the robot not to let the target out of site and not to let him forget about that one.

There would always be something and benjamins dun flowers would always tell benjmain who had been

aboard while he ws on te planet not that the spirit five had many visitors.
While Benjamin in ws busy doing his business his mission nobody actually knew what they were they for although they were the robots companions.

Benjmain paranoia finally sets a side as he boards the space ship awaiting lucy s arrival as tey were both being checked out by the planets guards basically the air port police. As lucy has to explain and the guards miss understanding lucy until benjmain intervenes.

Once all in the clear after being told by benjmain to let her pass with the robot they were all bound and on their way back to the planet earth just to drop lucy back home. Again as lucy ws going to re live some of her old memory's.

She ws feeling a little nervous, benjmain tells her that he would be close and that she should keep hold of the spirit five badge in case of any trouble, they both agree within the four hours in and through the mind they are back on the planet earth this time it was two weeks..

Lucy stays of the space ship she is in the same old hotel they both laugh as they remember as Benjamin was by her side. They had been there before.
As lucy is close to tears benjmain is congratulating her on her bravery benjmain tells her tat he would be close. And with the power of his badge disappears only to disappear completely.

The first thing lucy does is to throw her self down on a hotel well-made bed she had spend quite a long time sleeping standing up right. It ws the same room and the same smell. She was down stairs also once again not so cosy but safer and out of the public eye.

It looked like benjmain had made a deal with the owner and lucy through that ws in business. Lucy was free and could have anything that she wanted for the next two weeks. Her bed ws a single one neatly made looking comfortable.
Lucy get up off the bed still remaining the first time that she had stayed there and the mouse hole that ws there in the room the last time tat she had stayed there had been filled in. lucy shudders with the thought. Remembering where the fridge was lucy s goes to open it and to her surprise there ws some beer probably left over from her last stay. In the fridge with a welcoming card too with she had left for her self. Lucy smiles saying that while thinking about benjmain who was nice and close to her nearby.

Lucy did not think again and is busy now opening a couple of beers. They were in date which surprised her even more. As lucy cheers her self as she gets on to her bed and laying down as she thanks benjamins again as she opens another beer. As lucy puts her feet up and is finally relaxing.
Meantime benjmain is feeling the pressure as he ahd not told lucy the real truth, as he was in town also now for two reasons one to make sure that lucy got some real time off and rest and then two to make sure that they both hit the target.

Benjmain sends lucy a message that she ahs to watch her own back for a while a more than a few minutes in fact twenty minutes. Giving her the details lucy is content and is keeping her cool. The robot and benjmain sends a message to the NYPD which in return sent a messages to the CPD, The cyber police department.

Benjamin hears through the grapevine that about a little Italians guys arrest had blown his cover. And a new case had been opened, lucy ws now being watched not just by benjmain but by the cyber police it ws the first time that Lucy's identity had been known to the police on the earth. Benjmain could see trouble coming from all distance's.
He was not particularly happy with the news. She was being watched not now just the spirit five but now by the oxygen and the hitman. The cyber police.

This new approach was making things for the spirit five team more complicated it ws the first time that the tables had changed it looked like benjamins team were actually in trouble real trouble for once even though benjmain still had time to resolve his problems. Benjian needed to stop Lucy and the massager if that report of what they were doing gets in to te hands of the cyber police. Benjmain and his team and the spirit five would have to abort there mission.

Benjmain orders the computer to track the cops position he was being taken to jail. As he asks the robot if he had found them both then robot tell benjmain that he has made contact.

The robot tells benjmain that there target was in prison probably trying to protecting itself.
The robot tells benjmain that the target was in prison with the oxygen and the hitman guarding him.

Benjmain could see the future a mile away itv ws fact that oxygen and the hitman were trying to lure him in. benjmaij could play games too. As he speaks to his computer in and on the spirit five. As he uses it to describe there systems when things like these things happen gtgghe oxygen an the hitman have there records and benjmainis all over them.
The hitman thinks that it is his imagination the hitman knows it is benjmaij a miles off. the oxygen and the hitman made sure that it was only the both of them in the building with the benjmains target within the both of them the both of them both targets awaiting for a reaction.
There was not one.

Benjmain computer in the spirit five was closing in on the jails systems down, benjmais wants his ship to work faster and he tells the robot to work faster and he tells the robot to plug himself in if it helped.
As benjamins steps off his ship his space ship backed up and fully loaded with his badge.
Mean time lucy is at the casino rolling the dice on the robots behalf as lucy had been given her gold card as lucy cast off, not knowing that she was going to lose as the robot on the spirit five was fixing herb transactions. As benjmain tells the oxygen that he knows that he ws there and his presents was actually felt.

The oxygen calls out to the Benjamin telling him that there was know way that Benjamin was going to get the target that he was protecting.
Benjmain laughs that one off as he touches his spirit five badge transforming himself into the spirit five tiger. Benjamin roars loudly letting every know about his presents leaving the police men in silent. As te echo of Benjmains roar echoed through the building as he echoed his roar right throw the building as Benjamin make an entry.

Benjamin moves in slowly coolly he was taking his time. It would be mor sensible if the target had kept its self behind the bars of the jail. In fact due it was a bad discussions in that the target had chose to run. As benjmain approaches an empty jail cell, only to attach the smell of the targets after shave that he had left behind himself.
This had made things a little more easier for benjmain as he was still following all three of them by smell.

They were not to far off, as the smell of the target gets stronger benjmain is realizing them. Benjmain closes as for there whereabouts up stairs or down stairs the smell says that he was up stairs and benjmain was ready to oblige however benjmain believed that he was being misguided and continue to hunt his target down stairs.

The oxygen calls out to benjmain telling him that there ws no way that benjmain ws going to hey the target that he was protecting. Benjmain laughs that one off as he touches his spirit five badge transforming himself in to the tiger. Benjmain roars loudly the police men stand as the echo of benjmain roar echoed right through him and around the building as benjmain makes his entrance.

Benjmain moves slowly cool like coolly he ws taking his tome knowing what to expect he was taking his time it would have been sensible if the target had kept himself behind the bars of the jail. In fact die to the extremely bad discission the target had chose to run. As benjmain approaches the empty jail cell only to capture the smell of designer aftershave. That smelt like it had been there for days that looked like it had been left there this made things a little easier for benjmain because now he has a cent and would now track them by that smell.

They were not to far way as the smell of thee target gets stronger Benjmains is nearing them. Benjmain to has to make a discission weather to go up stairs or weather to stay down stairs the smell of the air around him ws leaving him to believe that the targets has split up. He could still smell the air the cent in both directions.

Benjmain makes the discissions to hunt them down stairs so he does.
As the oxygen has the target by his side and is in deep conversation with the man asking him exactly what did he doe to up set benjmain and he continued to the man it was not the kind of person that you would like to argue with. The man tells the hitman straight which was unusual as he was a coward and he ws lying.
The man continued that he was trying to follow some girl that's all you know the next minute you guys are surrounding me and I am here what's going on and who is that guy in the space suit.
What guy.
From know where benjamins appears picking the oxygen up by his throat and throwing him down wards on to the ground.

As he transforms into the tiger he steps Infront of the target both of them the hitman and the target. Who was not the actual target he ws some body who ws in the wrong place at the wrong time he was in danger just for following lucy around on her week off and shopping trip.

As benjmain growls in front of the man saying quite a few words and reminding him that if he tries to approach a member of his team he would pay. Benjmain continues if he ever touches a girl again your my next meal and benjmain tells him that he would be watching him so he had better be careful. He ends the conversation with do you understand me.
The man nods his head in agreement however it ws not over yet as benjmain asks the man to repeat what he had just said back to him.
As the oxygen goes to make a move on Benjamin, he roars again powerful enough to knock the oxygen off his feet. And further more in to the corner of the room. Benjmain roars once more he says again remembers he came in peace.
Say it, he continued.
The oxygen has no choice but to comply he repeats the words that benjmain had told him to. Benjmain disappears. The strange man is left in the cell with th oxygen just about being able to pick himself up of the floor and out of the corner of the cell. The oxygen a confused why the spirit five did not harm them.

That was the oxygens talking point of the day, with the hitman and the oxygen slowly listening to benjmain instead of themselves they have to question themselves aware they going to listen to the alien. Instead of the hitman and the oxygen in there own minds had to admire benjmain for his approach and as for the hunting of him the oxygen knows that benjmain was not a killer

as he had quite a few being made on the oxygen himself.
And like the spirit five had always said that there mission ws of one of peace. The oxygen was beginning to believe benjamin he did not speak about the experincves that he had been through with benjmain and refused to discuss his experiences wigth his ownpartner the hitman.
The hitman ha a totally different operson when it came down to speaking about benjmain and what they were doing on the planet earth. And of course why they were catually there.
What he did not know ws that he was employed to keep people safe on the earth. If that meant chasing benjmain so be it she says. As the oxygen explains to the hitman mind was else where he was watching and looking about the streets and waiting for a crime he needed some body to arrest.
Only to top his day off as he too now ws feeling hungry and was off to the burger van for a burger.
Asking the man quickly and politely if he could have a hot dog the man tells him yes. The oxygen tells the man to fill it right up.
With.
Tomatoes sauce and anything else you have behind your bar.

You got some cash.

I saw that one coming you do not have to act so tight.
Come on al I have is a card.
Ok
The oxygen looks hard in to his glove compartment removing his e=wallet he takes out a couple of dollars pushing them in to the hitman's hands and ask him to

pay the man through his window. Not because he did not want to get out of the car simply because he was in and on the drivers side closest to the van.

It was nice and lucy was nicely dressed in her new outfit, as she was standing at the hotel bar. Benjamin was jut finishing his other business and is on his way back to her.
The oxygen and the hitman had been observing what had been reported sitting of benjamins space craft the

spirit five had been seen there conversation was going one way as they already knew that benjmain had been on the [planet as for what the hitman and the oxygen just experienced.

The oxygen had not approached the hitman to explain that conversation and that he would have to explain earlier in the evening with benjmain.

Later on in the morning a guest arrives and an argument occurs about benjmain and the hitman as he was not particularly impressed as the oxygen was trying ton explain that he believed that Benjamin was harmless and he ws on there planet like he had said that he ws on a mission of peace. And his pledge's for and on the earth was to better them and the human race.

He continued that it was not there planet as he tries ton explain he continued that he needed to see somebody who was honest. He continues. As he comes up with the conclusion that the human race had destroyed enough of it as for this time. The hitman burst out laughing asking the oxygen if he needed ton see somebody. The hitman continued falling in love with aliens and a snotty little posh girl boy when I get out of this car im am going to have a really good look at you.

The oxygen knew that he had stepped over his mark and he continued well these a pause hitman he continued if you can not see the truth yet then you as well as everybody else are blinded he continued however he did not get an answer form his partner the hitman did not answer.

The hitman casually pulls over the cool one to the curb by the road edge. It ws a quiet street. He tells the oxygen to get out of the cool one the oxygen agrees and he gets out of the car the hitman follows him he to gets out of the cool one stepping on to the road. As the hitman follows the oxygen an argument starts. The disagreement went a little further than just words they both had the thought of fighting. Both of them in anger and both of them in the position to attack each other.

As the verbal disagreement had came to an end a stand still and neither of them anything to say. The oxygen is the first to get back inside of the cool one, followed quickly by this partner who tells him that he wanted to swap places as it was his turn to drive. As the oxygen and the hitman swap places both still in disagreement. Not just over the oxygens feeling but now the changing of there positions in the vercle.

By this time lucy ws nice and drunk and ws heading back down stairs to her make shift room and ws busy ordering herself some food in fact a lot of food and even more so plus some beer.

As she salutes benjmain with the beer and with out him by her side and drunk Ly shouting knowing that she ws so dar apart form benjmain he would not hear a thing. Again shouting the words benjmain to Benjamin she continued here's to space cheers ton another adventure. And lst of all cheers to my best friend in all of his world my robot. This behavoiur went on for more than a few minutes. It stopped when there was a knock at her door cheers to the knock at the door she continued.

As she opened the door grabbing a hand full of food off the table as it is being brought I to the room. The food was what she had ordered. As the half opened the door taking more food off the trolly and then finally letting the man into the room. As she looked around her room for her purse which she cannot find and quickly resolves it with stick it on my tab.
The man answers her of course however he ws still expecting a tip, as he stands there with his hand out. Lucy again thinking quickly as she had nothing available at that time scribbles on to a napkin that was on the tables tray and writes an IOU. Lucy then apposes throwing the man out of her room and swipes a beer off the trolly.

The man walks off with a graceful look upon his face.

The oxygen and the hitman were busy making friends with each other all over again and the oxygen he gets back to his normal level of friendliness agreeing that his troubles have left him in a muddle and it ws some thing that he would have to think about hard.

The hitman mind ws else where as his partner ws trying to apologies to him. The hitman was watching the sky's as he says to the oxygen who was busy pouring his heart out to the hitman he ws discussing something completely different the whereabouts of where abouts of where lucy and benjmain might be.

They had decided that they would leave things as they are for now. They had decided that they would leave things as they are to sit back for now. And theyb decided that they would watch the targets from a distance.

They had joined benjmain and the spirit five in watching lucy.
Benjmain was a sleep at the front of the spirit five as he was he was dreaming of he was dreaming about a normal earth life was slowly getting to him. Benjmain had not told lucy that he had or was becoming more jealous over the fact that she ws a human. And had ernt the prillivage of being aloud to walk freely not just on her planet but his also.

He did not and it ws made clear by the silhouette a master a destroyer of all humans beings and when he gets the chance and is subjected by the rules of the badge as he tries to obey his commanders the council of lou he would only appear to them and them only.
The conversation with the silhouette and the council was a quick one as quick as Benjmains as he knew that he was being spoken by him he might just turn up which was what had happened before lucky it ws just Benjmains mind left asleep and dreaming.
As benjmain wakes he awakes as if he was defiantly himself and in a fight and with a jump is up right shutting the words get off me. With a little feeling of being in shock it was clear not only to benjmain but the team he clearly had some problems with his sleep.

As benjmain is nice and awake he calls to his robot who was doing all the watching at that time.
As he moves from his seat to another with a camera as benjmain walks in asking him shy he ws being ignored the robot moves form Benjmains seat and sits next to him in the co pilots seat.

Benjmain was half asleep at the front the helm of the spirit five he is still dreaming as he try's to do other things. Both of them are now watching lucy as the robot continues still in control while talking to the computer benjmain thinks that the approach was going to happen in the evening however things would be made harder if the target was to make a move during the day. This was not a good thing for the spirit five crew. As they all preferred to do there business in the evening, at night time.

Benjmain does not know yet tat he had been exposed it was the thought he had totally forgotten about. What he had done to the man that was following lucy. Forgetting about 0oxygen and the hitman that was his only mistake as they had not forgotten about him. And they were closer to benjmain as he had thought.

Benjmain has parked his space ship in the near by park near the nearest hotel. Benjmain new already that he has some seriously expensive taste. And now that money was no option as the robot could hack its self in to all kind of places. The opportunity that had come that it would be there for taking was one of an abundant one.

However that pacific evening lucy was back at the casino rolling dice this time around. Benjmain was watching her trying to figure it out what all of the excitement was all about of what lucy ws doing he did not think to much about the power of money.

Lucy was rolling the dice and benjmain catches on reminding the robot to make the changes tat they had agreed upon. The robot was making the changes that he would start to lose, on the other end of things lucy unexpectedly catches on. Benjmain is surprised. As she drops about eight hundred pounds within a few minutes she knew her luck ws out.
She leaves the table thinking that it ws an extremely large change in luck she suspecting something. However she takes the thought no further than the lady's rest room. The toilets were full and lucy did not seem to care as she leaves the lady's room to go in to the men's instead as the lady's were full and the gentlemen's were empty. And as well as surprising some people comes out of the bathroom and back straight on to another table.

Lucy stay's around not knowing yet that her team up stairs in the space ship were watching her. Not yet knowing that she ws being used as bate. As there was some free drinks being past around champagne lucy decide s to stay around.
Benjmain was wishing that he could be human ihe says to the robot that they seem to have a lot oof fun with

out any care. The topic was one of fun and the subject arises more than once as they watch her play. At seemed this week was one of dreams.

Ws benjmain beginning to weaken to the human way of life as he knows that there was no fault. Was benjmain losing his mind had he over spent his time on the planet earth. Or ws benjmain just being benjmain. Benjmain wanted to be part of the e action and the council were they forcing them to stick to there plans by them, there was no chance of benjmain journey. Lucy was down stairs in the bars and in the casino rooms

The robot knew benjmain feeling about what ws going on, he approaches benjmain telling him he has his back and if he wanted to get closer to her it could be made possible. He could make the agreements.
Benjmain had thought about what the robot had said he ws still managing just to fight her feeling s of wanting total piece of the action. He said to the robot that he would continue to watch. Once a persons in danger and not knowing there in danger enough he continued that it was lucy that he needed to protect and she knows that hse is good. The robot intervenes as it interrupts that is not the way she is going to act when she finds out we set her up. We will all betaking another holiday on your behalf.

Benjmain smiles the robot insists again that it ws not funny benjmain tells the robot that his smile was one of thanks and one of jealously it could be one of happiness or even anything benjmain apologises. And a few words later telling the robot that his behaviour was a little bit out of character.

Benjmain continuing his normal self asks the robot to switch places with him the robot agrees they both shift positions. He continues just to keep watching her the robot does as it is told.
Benjamin is fast asleep dreaming of what believes is the future, the images are that of he dreams are collected by the robot and are later discussed. So that they could be analysed in the near future on Benjmains planet where they would be discussed by the council of Lou in the city of Lou.

In benjmain world different places leave him to believe that there would be different futures and so on.
Benjmain is dreaming about lucy it is a good dream.
And it was a good time to dream about her we think this because there had been a time where when benjmain had nothing but nightmares way back on his -planet his dreams were of the silhouette at that time and not forgetting that he too came from the earth, before he became a protected. After he destructs the silhouette only for the council to bring him back.
Benjmain did not know that his dreams were just about to change, as for the first couple of weeks benjmain keeps the change in him to himself the robot was the first to notice as it was just him on the spirit five. It was told to him by the sunflowers they would hear lots but they would never say a word. Unless the robot talks to them as they were his friends.
The sunflowers were cleaver they too knew noticed the change in his behaviour and his real feelings.

When they were happy they would stand up right nice and tells and when they were saddened they would stop as if they had been let down or hurt of they could tell if benjmain was in a good mood. And in good health and like vise versa.

The robot noticed the sun flowers and has to ask them some questions in flowers language about what they think has been going on as he shows them some signs of stress and tiredness and a few other things. The robot check's benjamins suit for him and his own safety running dialysis everything's looks fine food intake and body fuiled good according to the suit your fine as fore the second opinion benjmain was not fine the robot insists that they should leave. Benjamin jumps telling and reminding lucy that they were half way through there mission.

The robot tells benjmain to look at him closely if you do not get the right treatment you will die. Benjmain knows that he is in trouble. What about lucy? He shy's away lucy can live here on the earth until you arrive again. That's not what I want to her. Benjamins answers him feeling the siut slowly drain what's left of the suit's energy.
Ok we can abort the missioned leave the silhouette to the cyber cops I mam sure that they would take the pleasure and have more time and fun. However we can not leave lucy on her own.
The robot again says look at him the girls stays on the planet weather we like it or not. Benjmain gets jealous quickly as he continues that it was his mission not there's not the silhouette's the robot tells benjmain he really understands him and asks him to look at him again. Its your choice

Benjmain needs time to think the robot tells him that there's nothing to think about they would pick up lucy in the morning and drop of==her off later on in the day then your free and we can get you back home.

We will not be seen or be heard and we are heading back to LOU just for a few days in your mind Benjamin it will feel like a few hours. Come on benjmain you know already that it's the right decision
Benjmain looking hard for answers gives in and shows it by the look on his face ok he says that's the plan. Ok put the cloak on take me down on to the earth and park we can wait there until I have a chance to speak with lucy. She will not be to angry we will wait there until I speak to her and collect lucy she is not going to be happy as it is her break.
It was not her holiday.

They both look at each other.

It is late in the evening and lucy is dressed up dancing on the dance flor with another human only for her to look up and see benjmain standing there. Nobody noticed the unorthodox dress his pace siut, lucy did. Benjmain makes an approach not to lucy likening as she ws drunk and it ended up looking like her dad had come to pick her up early benjmain being the farther and doing the collection. As lucy is dragged off. benjmain has collected her and is telling her there has been a change of plan. She was going with him.

Lucy finally stops playing a round and agrees apologising as she tells benjmain that it was tat she ws drunk it happens all the time you know with parents and there children that sort of thing. Benjamín looks at her lucy looks back with a silent sorry. Lucy ws finally understanding as she is dragged off further even with people watching her looking at her.
As she is she asked benjmain a question one ws are they in danger benjmain answers quickly yes all the time lucy says like now benjmain a=says yes like now. What was the excuse and why did you do that. I was

having fun, lucy stops again sorry she say that was a pint. Benjmain confused continues as they walk back to the park. By this time Benjamin had her by his hand and was dragging her off in to the spirit five. Close by the nearby park.

Once lucy had a shower and tidied her self up ready once again to join her team benjmain explains his situation with the suit. And why he has to leave the planet earth as well as her.
They did not tell her any more than that. Lucy spent the rest of the evening settling down and speaking long complicated conversations with te robot. Well he tells her it is good to be back. The robot tells lucy that she ws being re issued instated, they both smile lucy takes a seat.

Benjmain talks to his computer asking it to calculate time, as he believes if they move fast enough they could get to the city of Lou and back to new York city in well time.
Even though benjmain had fallen by his suit he ws well engrossed in making a good recovery and wanted to spend some time on the earth with the robot studying it. The robots discission was a good one and it came at a good time but an awkward time.

The suit its self could not be removed or taking off which the right equipment unless benjmain was on his own planet he would still ned to use the badge. Which ws another problem all together a totally different subject.

It would be a few days Benjmain would arrive with the spirit five however within his mind it would only be a few hours also. Benjmain ws back on his planet the planet of Lou.
Simply for the reason that his suit had failed and with out his space suit in the earth and is his space ship he would not and could not survive. It was Lucy's turn to be a leader and she calls the shots for benjmain who had fallen he had fallen poorly through the journey and ws trying his hardest to be and look normal. It was going to be an imbaresing moment for benjmain he did not want anybody to know.
the thought of Benjamin being poorly was making himself feel weak. Lucy could feel Benjmains sadness over the whole thing and on the subject and the robot still thinking that the badge did not work and only suggested tht he ws apart of the spirit five team.
This smiles benjmain as the robot with his badge as the robot had forgotten that his badge did not do to much as for when it is doing impressions of Benjamin tapping his badge and speaking the words spirit five especially somethings had change him in to something he gets nothing but disappointment while leaving benjmain smiling.

Until Benjamin is jabbed by a doctor who was putting benjmain to sleep as for his laughter it had soon stopped.
Benjmain ws now busy being reprepared, the problem was that a pin head split or a pinhead hole in his suit naked to the human eye and only visible by the computer states his suit himself and the robot could know about this. However none of them would be able to see the damage. To see what the problem was. Even so it was found by benjamins quick thinking. His suit ws being switched he ws I the right place. Prepared and made right in front of him.

Benjmain is waiting to try on his knew suit there had been a few changes concerning the badge there was a new one.
This did not worry benjmain to much just one more suit to power up. He thought. He could handle it he lied he says to lucy looking at her inwardly like to say with the extra poser in the suit was not part of the deal even so it was too late for benjmain to change his mind the suit had just been remade in front of him and was on his body.
A normal person would of probably excepted the extra power for battle. Benjmain had not stopped talking all the way back to the planet earth. Lucy ws quite as benjmain seemed excited now that he would draw trouble towards him, lucy thought other wise and

benjmain started up a new discussion about the knew suit and badge.
He was talking a lot and lucy could not get a word in she was quiet benjmain knew that he would have to try and run a check in the near future it was going to be on the planet earth.

Chapter 4

With a new badge everything else ws put a side and it was the topic of the conversation. All four of them were discussing the new phenomenon it was like the spirit five being returned to its normal self. With benjmain and lucy the robot and the computer with the sunflowers were all eye to use it and found out how the suit works and find out how good the new suit and badge was going to be.

Benjmain settles the spirit five way down at the bottom of the ocean. There was no change at that moment Benjamin ws down there for a few days still the badge had no response. Benjamin was deep in conversation with lucy telling her that it cannot be right he decides to take the spirit five up wards upon to atmosphere above the planet. Close and near the ozone.

As Benjamin does this he is thinking hard about the decisions that he as made and really wanted the badge to work if any at all as neither anybody in his team were just there to experience it any thing that the new badges powers.

Benjamin was confused lucy was the same as they both waiting for the badge to transform them in to something. Again benjmain was thinking hard an asks lucy if she had heard right as the badges seemed to be in the same positions at least that ws right and correct some thing they were doing ws wrong as they cannot seem to understand how there new badges would boot in to there suits and badge power.

Benjmain knows himself and his crew was just going to have to figure it out by themselves. In fact according to lucy ut was a rule they had no choice as benjmain explains and continues they take the space ship from the ozone above the planet down to the earth and land nice and coolly at midnight in the forest.

Lucy ws a little disappointed having her holiday cut a little short which some how became a topic and conversation of the early morning, on the space ship on the spirit five. Benjmain was neither here or there he had other things on his mind. As well as for what ws going on down on the earth.

It had taken them two weeks just to figure out exactly how the suits work lucy ws surprised with all the attention. She thought that it ws only benjmain s who ws issued a new suit and when she finally gets her on she says to benjmain that it felt incredible. Benjmain half disagreed.
They both ahd changed the spirit five outfit was no longer just blue it ws now blue and white it felt comfortable both lucy and benjmain agree. And as for its power they were pretty much the same. The thought of it ws incredible and as the changes were made to suit to suit his mind. This was even better as benjmain talks to lucy who was slowly created a suit that actually suited there needs.

They get to chose the powers they wanted depending now on what kind of thoughts they were receiving the most appreciated thoughts benjmain and lucy were both taking part in what had become an experiment. They were making the spirit five space suit.

The spirit five would still be the same except more powerful that also it would only apply to benjmain and Lucy's space suit's they had there own powers pretty much the same again just a little more powerful as the space ships computer was awarded with telepathy. Lucy ws not sure weather this was for the good or the bad. However it had been done.
Lucy was in self denile as she did not know what to think with being gifted with her new suit and powers of her choice. Meantime benjmain was loving it and believed that this would be as good as the old one even better he thought.

The hitman and the oxygen were in a conversation in confusion in how the two space criminals the elite as the oxygen called them manages to escape them again. The hitman only tells the oxygen that it would only be a matter of time before he makes a move on the girl lucy it would be just a matter of time when she would slip up. He continued that it ws true. The hitman really believed in his.

He says it again tat it was just a matter of time. She will fall he continued.
The oxygen looks confused and the hitman was just about to start teasing him as he makes a move by talking to the computer and the cool one.
The oxygen was feeling weird after the long conversation about the spirit five team he was slowly convincing himself that the spirit five team were of goodness and were here. The oxygen knew that if that ws true he would need evidence. And on top of that he would need to prove it to his partner the hitman.

The oxygen was questioning himself as he wanted to explain what he was thinking to the hitman his own theory's of why they were there not them but the spirit five team.

The oxygen needed to level things out with the hitman he was beginning to think tht the three team mates up above them there to do a job.

the oxygen was thinking that he was or had some crazy as he is interrupted by the hitman who was waiting for the opportunity to tell the oxygen about the way he ws feeling about the whole things of having the spirit five down on the planet earth.

The hitman starts the conversation it ws normally the other away around. The hitman conversation ws unexplained by the hitman he continued to fire question after question at the oxygen. Just answer my questions he said and ill set you free. The oxygen answers his first question

The oxygen continued how did you know tat he had feeling for the spirit five team and changed. The hitman answered it almost straight away. And that it had been under water for the last three months regards to the spirit five.

As for the second the oxygen believed that was similar leading the hitman that the oxygen was telling him the truth. And they were on the earth to resolve its problems. The hitman gives the oxygen the ok he says to him tat his word was feasible. It had made sense. However it was not over yet the last question that they were all waiting to hear even though it made no difference and had no confidants however this time they both agreed that it ws a mission of peace. The forth question was not there with the fifth question they did not exists as there ws no further fault so they could not exists.
Now the oxygen still had to answer the question which ws it sane to be following benjmain around ws it actually legal and if so was he going to quite and give up his badge.

The hitman reminds the oxygen that people in the modern world do not have feeling like that. And if I was you if I was living those types of feelings then I would be careful of who you are talking to.
The oxygen wanted a pint of beer after having a long debate of why and when and about why he was thinking like that. He was thinking that benjamins his crew could actually be there alive on the planet earth. The hitman was always up for the debate he ws harden by the oxygens thoughts but only just agreeing with some of the things he said.

Out of nowhere comes an array of words the hitman verbally destroys the oxygens conversation a verbal fight had begun. The oxygen had lost by a few sentences neither of them would stop this ws normal as cyber police they would do this not a bit but a lot. That was one of the reasons that they were partners together, by there boss.

The hitman still up set an running out of things to say as he is keeping the oxygen close to him.
On a level and in his mind the oxygen had not told the hitman about his true feelings about the way he had felt about lucy and benjmain, as for the fact that they ahd been acquainted through there meetings and in battle. the hitman still listening while being at or should I say on top of things as the oxygen is dreaming about the spirit five team. The hitmans feeling were just the same as they were he was willing to approach the oxygen again on the subject.

A conversation starts which is blown out of proportion as the two cyber police open a conversation which they should not have done speaking about a subject that they were warned that they should avoid.
The hitman was angry and was extremely against what the oxygen ahd said. They did not care that there planet earth ws being watch over by another planet. And that they were all totally not interested in it to make it safer for there race the human race that default upon it form time. There conversation had started it ws not going to be a couple of lines or a couple of minutes in fact it went form a single sentence in to a small argument in to

a conversation in to there bosses office and from there on go the street yes things worked that fast. It ws less than an hour before the word was out. To the spirit five. Benjmain heard the message he was really surprised as it looked like the humans were finally realizing what they had done and now trying to resolve it and reverse the change and reverse te danger of losing there planet completely.

The hitman would not be getting off easy there were many thins tat would have to be put in place.
Even though the human s had realized the council in the city of Lou were still not convinced and the council still wanted to destroy the earth. Benjmain was staying put telling the council that his mission was nearly over and he was ready to come back home.

Meantime lucy was questioning benjmain they were heading back to the earth and lucy seemed to be in praises as she was nice and happy. Which was not just noticed by benjmain but the robot and the sunflower's also.
The robot and lucy was acting really different and benjmain wa s waiting for her to make her move she ws obviously thinking about some thing which was keeping her happy. Which ws keeping a smile on her face.
Finally lucy tells benjmain why she was laughing while about him it was because it was lucy s birthday benjmain smiles and is surprised telling her that she had

kept that quiet. Not letting him know when in fact he had not forgotten and he was waiting for his robot to find her records as evidence.

Lucy could not stop smiling and it ws her space crew for that day. The robot takes the helm telling benjmain to switch seats, a mutrel l request that they did this with out arguments.

If the robot needed to take control of the spirit five it had the authority to do so.
The robot takes the space ship down onto the planet earth, lucy was told to dress smart she questioned him also only for benjmain to walk out nice and smart lucy and benjmain were going out to party just for one evening. Lucy ws going to get the gift again of acting normal.

Benjmains party begins and ends with a trouble as always lucy ws drunk again benjmain ws close by her picking up the pieces as lucy's drunken approach did not seem to impress anybody and in the end ending up in the girl's bathroom in tears.
As benjmain thinks that it is all clear just girl stuff before he enters the bathroom as for te state that lucy ws in she was crying and telling benjmain as he locks the lady rooms by leaning back wards on the door explains to lucy that life that's what its all about and that's the way its always going to be.
Lucy give benjamins cheeky get lost its her birthday.

Lucy has to explain why she was in that mood she said tht everybody was making fun of her and she did not know what to think. As her tears start over again she rushes back into the bathroom this time getting in to the toilet cubical and locking the door shut.
This was weird benjmain thought. Benjmain was getting a new image of who lucy actually was.

Not only was lucy fully pledged part of the spirit five team she was also very caring enough to speak and speak honestly these four things were part of her personality. Benjmain had just noticed them, not even in benjmais relationship had he showed that much of himself to lucy. The robot and benjmain had started to study lucy again and were taking notes.

Benjmain ws now well awear of lucy out of character behaviour she did not show it too to many people l and benjmain knows now she can change. While on the space ship with benjmain there ws a question was lucy really hiding part of her personality or was it just nothing and benjmain was excited about Lucy's behaviour counting out that she was actually drunk when this behaviour had started.

Benjmain reasons and in his thoughts decides that it ws just part of Lucy's ego. She ws very lucky. And before that, he was talking to her making it clear tat lucy ws just lucy there ws no in-between or second person and as her mind it ws clean.

Even so benjmain wanted to know even more she suggested that tey go back to there planet of lou and discuss it with his council benjmain corrects her there council.
Benjmain agree for tat moment that she ws an earthling s and that's how they behave. He was listening to lucy and had not missed a word as lucy was really laying it

on. Not just to get her point across but to make sure that everybody who was about her heard. Slightly out side of Lucy's character but it ws done. Lucy finally gets her point across, as both herself and benjmain they went off for a dance. As lucy leads on the dance floor once there is room benjmain follows her into the next dance which was coming up slowly.

Chapter 5

Benjmain breaks the ice as they dance it looked like lucy had pulled through as for her emotional side of her thoughts they both enjoyed what they were doing as for benjmais he to enjoyed the flirting. And ws watching how normal she was. To benjmain surprise lucy ws good especially brushing off porter dancers which were men on the dance floor.

Other people were watching her and she seemed to pull a crowed right in front of her people around them both and it looked like benjmain had some how done the same as he too finds himself within a crowed area on the dance floor. Some how being pulled part by the dance. Both disappears in to separate crowds.
Only to find each other a few minutes later as the music stops and the next song comes on with out stopping. Benjamin was hers for that evening, as lucy continue to dance more people were showing an interest and she was not wearing her spirit five badge or in her space suit yet and as for benjmain it would only take some body an earthling to look at them both funny and he would get up set.

He could still change as he still had his badge lucy had not yet ernt that right if benjmain pleased he would change from his tuxedo to his space suit and so on through his new space suit powers. However on this occasion he was keeping himself cool.

Lucy was thinking about mars and benjmain was thinking about Venus, as they both split and disappear through the crowd on the dance floor lucy is still dancing still pulling all her moves off. while Benjmains had found the bar waiting upon Lucy's arrival. Benjmain not being able to consume human foods and

Lucy gets there just in time to get her drinks in. one for the nearest girl and then one for her self.
With benjmain and lucy both keeping there s eyes on each other everything was running smoothly and as the evening leaves and the night time renews its it self. It becomes the morning and the end of Lucy's birthday. They meet and greet each they were not to far away at the end of te night they take a slow walk back to the park. And to the spirit five space ship.

For some strange reason benjmain had taken to the country side, on the planet earth he found that it gave him a feeling of peacefulness and it ws a place where he could think. However right now his business was in the city. Soon he would make some time to re visit it the country side some time next time he was available.

Lucy and the robot who's name was DARYL. All thought the same. And all had the same thought of peace and peace full thoughts.
Benjmain and lucy were thinking about the earth thinking tat it may serve them a purpose that was not benjamins wishes he was beginning to sound like the council. Lucy rephases what she had said. What she meant to say ws that the earth could go on an serve its purpose to the people on the earth.

It would be a lesson learnt benjmain said however benjmain already knew the future of the planet earth in the million years before it to come.
The hitmans race has a purpose of destroying everything that they were given including people benjmain closes his eyes his thoughts were racing and benjmain needed to calm himself down.

As lucy comes to the ned of her birthday she was left with all the love an silliness feeling happy then upset in places and as drunk as much as before she had started. As she could possible be.
the robot and the sunflower were laughing at lucy as lucy ws trying to question them and they knew tat she knew that they would only answer the robot as they were his. As they say nothing lucy tells them to birth shut up. They were not talking any how.

As the robot is close repeating lucy in the mood for a conversation as she tries to talk a little drunk and to drunk to answers the robots question as for the two sunflowers. The robot gets upset as he thinks lucy is trying to speak with them and she is. The robot is protective of them.
Benjmain is busy observing things he had noticed before they ahd left the park where they were hiding and waiting for Lucy's arrival previously before there plans had changed a strange man had pulled up in the park area parked near the space ship he ws cloaked however the spirit five as a space ship was one of the best and the computer on board finds the ships signals. It lets the robot know of its presents it ws clear to benjmain that they ahd a visitor it was the silhouette.

Lucy ws to drunk to comment and benjmain was armed and amazed a it looked like it ws some more action.

Within a few minutes of them of them arriving they had taken off again and it looked like it was just a drop off.

Once again the whole thing seemed familiar benjmain never forgot a face and it looked like it ws a wise who was claiming to be a tough guy. Benjmain was unimpressed then impressed even though submission as he wanted to know the mans business on the planet as he came out of a space craft it was very unusual that he would of met the man twice.

He was now convinced that the man in question was looking for his head to be bitten straight off, cleanly straight off. as benjamin could feel the man he was of no structure unimportant a week person playing the big game a week human the strange man looks up wards slams his car door closed it was as if he was looking straight at benjmain right through the space ships cloak. Which was supposed to be impossible I fact it was.

Benjmain and the spirit five crew were there as the an had no idea that they were there. Benjmain needed to make sure.

Benjmain explains to the robot tht lucy is unavailable, as the strange man drives off, benjmain is questioning why he was there and if he should follow in pursue him as they ahd met for the third time.
It was impossible that benjmain would know him they were total stranger's, and benjmain has no evidence that he ws interfering with there mission. But he ws concerned by them meeting once then meeting him again unconsciously then meeting the man in the park. Who was this strange man.

Lucy shouts in a drunken manor she ws even more drunk as she had found some more beer in her fridge. That it ws coincidence bad timing on the clients behalf and bad timing for them the spirit five team. It was just bad luck ok benjmain agrees he ws not going to blow the whole thing open out of proportion, lucy agreed and then agreed again, lucy tells te computer that the man ws not to far away.

The computer joins in making an electronic signals and attaches it into the mans car and then the man himself. Benjmain needs an excuse to land back at the hotel. The robot could see benjmain was struggling do for an excuse and he has the same problem as he wants to intervene Benjamin is thinking DARYL. Had found an answer and bows out with a suggestion leaving the rest of the conversation with benjamins as they both made a mess of it. Lucy on the other hand was still drunk and it ws early I the morning. she says nothing as she did not understand what decision both teams were going to make.

Benjmain knew tat he ws going to have to come clean and lucy finds out that he not going tom like it, it was time for benjmain to see how cool she really was. Lucy ws nice a quiet and everybody
Moving the other two away so that they were in the distance as for the robot DARYL. Who would normally fake a sicky to pull lucy it was just another one of her games to her almost straight away lucy had noticed and as she did benjmain and lucy realises what she had forgot making it look like benjmain had hidden something. It did not take lucy to long to figure it out. She ws up for the confrontation it started with her approaching Benjmains while he was floating around the spirit five.

As she joins in telling benjmain that he had some thing to tell her, benjmain ws playing it cool however it was supposed to be the other away around, er no nothing as such what's up. Lucy continued oh I see respect and respect why are we still on this planet. Benjmain is trying to understand her approach.

There ws a long silence from Benjamin and then nothing else as the cells are for his robots back up systems as lucy ws now going red with imbaresment and the robot DARYL did not turn up and used his only excuse that he was to also busy being charged benjmain shouts I am a little bit disappointed with you DARYL, the robot says nothing and lucy is free to question the both of them Benjmains looking for excuses.

Lucy continued that she was being set up as she tries to speak to benjmain and he us trying his hardest not to lie to her and tells he would explain as soon as she is sober as she insist that she had come down off the booze an hour again but still standing in front of the both of them the robot and himself holding a can of beer. As she takes a swig telling them well nearly. Ah guys come on.

There was no answer from any of them benjmain was in a corner as she is tying to explain what he had tried to do with her lucy was speaking to her self quietly prodding benjmain an slowly prodding him hard and harder. Benjmain knew that he has no excuses he could of told her and he should of told her.

His only excuse as at that time was that time came from the robot who lucy realises that they were both in it together and they were. Lucy goes off to have a word with the robot come on DARYL how much do you know. The robot claims that he ws still charging and prompts her to look and ask for benjmain. As he points sending her back. She continued that it ws ok and that he could tell her. Please give me something its is cleartext you two are both lying your in it and your in it too. It is obvious.
What if it ws my birthday all over again would you tell me then. So we will all lie to her about that and why we are really here lucy continues really in tears.

Lucy I do not want to say in hab turned up and screwed up I thought it would have been safer if we did not tell you to protect you benjmain says lucy ws listening and ws still upset that her best friend could of told her benjmain continued again that it a was to protect her.

Benjmain continued that he did ot want to hurt her feelings and the opposite had happened. Benjmain is busy really trying hard not to push the conversation back I his direction in to an argument because that s what he does not want it to be.
Lucy ws asking him some complicated questions. Benjamín just about had the mind to answer them. Benjmain has to tell her straight that he was using her because it ws to keep thigs simple she would be his cover while he made the hit. And it was supposed to be closure and that it would have been better that she did not know you did not know. That's why you had no edivence tht you knew because you did not know about any hit of the target.

Lucy is surprised and continued to benjmain that she wanted to hear the rest. Your council out there still do not trust me benjmain tells her to wait it was not about trust it was about the hit they made the plans we have to stick by it and them. Lucy continued the space company still does not like humans. Benjmain says it she ws lucky and benjmain tells her once more that he has her back. Lucy says like wise I've got yours but you could have been a little more honest about the situation. And we are partners do not forget it.

The badge and the suit they mean nothing for me as form now lucy benjamins says I am sorry. Sorry does not come to it benjmain we are a team we work together. Benjmain Lucy's says you better start writing me out an apology. And take your time because it's a long way down there and if you cannot exists down in the planet earth im going down there. Benjian knew that she ws upset. And he did not know that she had meant it an the did not know how to apologise. He ws hoping that he could be good enough to talk her around in fact it ws another one of benjamins ideas which worked the other away around.

Benjmain continued an did not want to hurt her feeling s any further as the opposite had happened benjmain is trying hard and it came to the point a=that they both had said enough was lucys words to him as she tells him benjmain politely if she could shut up. Benjmain knowing that about in five minutes she ws going to burst and start shouting.
And about to lose her temper within a few m]seconds lucy lets go benjmain could do nothong and the robot was still charging on purpose. A few minutes later she was smashing up everything and anything she could find while floating around on the space ship suddenly everything gioes quiet benjmain and the robot think they are in the clear and lucy had finished.

Lucy voice echoed around the space ship do you want some more. Lucy was really up set. Lucy had just finished and was sitting on her bunk she is cooling down nicely and when benjmain approaches her nice and calmly tells her that she would be on report until

the damages that she has done is fixed and in working order.
She agrees with a half of an apology as benjmain cuts he rout of the conversation. There ws no apology's on the spirit five.

Benjmain explains to the rest of the team that lucy has given them apology and benjmain not forgetting her that she would also be giving the council of Lou an apology once back in front of the council. everything is by the book. He came up with the idea of using her as bate. Tere fore it too now was Benjmains turn to feel the pressure as he would have to explain to his council they were going home again.
The space journey was pretty much the same lucy was asleep and the robot was doing most of the flying. Wit the robot taking control of the journey there was a few bumps every couple of hours enough to disturb lucy s and benjamins sleep. As they awake believing that they had reached the planet of lou however this ws not the case as they were now navigating themselves in the spirit five through an asteroid belt. Saturn did no longer exist neither did mars the only other planted in the earths solar system was breathable air.

The first things was to do as for the spirit five team would to be why they had not moved as they were supposed to be on there wat home. Nobody could explain an d the second was why were they still in the earths solar systems. It was lucky tat they flew cloaked.

Maybe the humans got fed up by themselves and just blew the planets up themselves. Getting back home form where they were would now be a longer mission however going back to the last question it was not impossible taking back to the subject of the asteroids field that it was not as dence as they thought and they could manure about it what ws left of Saturn. It ws only recently that the planets ahd been removed as for the debris.
There ws no way around the mess and it looked like the robot was going to have to guide the space ship around it and eventually through it.

Benjmain takes it to heart he thinks he some how could of prevented it. Benjmain blames himself thinking that he some how started the destruction of the two planets. Some thing the planet earth and its people would not be able to handle.

Chapter 6

Benjmain awakes first as they approach the planet of lou heading straight to the base the robot is ijn control as the robot lands the first the spirit five hit the ground like a hunk of junk. Benjmains condition ws not a good one. The team was a little shaken by the robots landing.

Lucy did not notice until the last minute while they were docking the space craft the spirit five had minimal damage but needed some attention.
Meantime benjmain is taken back ton the doctors the same doctor that fixed him up last time he was in the city. The robot knew two procedures and was in a rush benjmain had lost consciousness he was in a coma. Benjmains space team were even more shocked when they find out that benjmain space suit was the problem they both get themselves checked out.
Lucy was in two minds and is talking to her self as she speaks the words do I really trust these people.
Lucy continues under some kind of machine. As she was the first to strip down she was feeling like child feels when they are asked by the doctor what is wrong. It ws like taking her very first shower. The robot plugs himself in. they both get themselves checked out. As for benjmain he had his suit built in to his systems it controlled everything his was attached to his brain. This time benjmain agrees that he should run the test. That he had forgotten to run when he ws there last.

Once again benjmain had to visit the council of lou and as he ws already there was no point in wasting time afters a couple of weeks in the city on the planet of lou which only ended up as a few hours to question Lucy's question was how he was being used by them as for being there bate a as the complained that if she was put at the plan she should have been told the arguments starts.

The council was my very first answer to making benjmain and lucy feel out of place benjmain assure s himself and lucy that it would be a quick questioning. As part of the plan ws two ask lucy some questions benjmain was just as good as them and was backing lucy all the way prompting her as they took to the courts room s questioning. As and before there councils raises there voices lucy ws well in to taking them for their rights to be on the council in the first place.

With Benjmains close and the silhouette nearby about them getting involved late lucy kept her head and continued to speak the conversation ws of a good nature and leaseing to listen too. No arguments an she lets the councillor's discuss her freely showing another peaceful part of lucy. And talking about her position and her future position within the spirit five.

The conversation went from lucy being praised to Lucy being questioned extremely fast and hard. When the questions start coming lucy is having trouble keeping up with all the news questions. She realizes that they are not playing games. The council were my first answers making benjmain and lucy feel out of place it was actually benjamins home. Benjmain adores there style of quick questioning.

Was part of there plan to keep lucy talking about things she would never had known the council with benjmain were close to the silhouette. About turn as they continued to speak to each other. The conversation was not a good one as they were talking about a person and there possible positions I the future. The silhouette wanted lucy.
The converstion went from an convincing friendly talk to an full blown up argument until weapons were drawn and another a battle commences a small one. As lucy watches with excitement as much as surprised and just as exciting agreeing and not knowing what she was agreeing too. And not realizing what had been said. As benjmain in suspires that still he mia understands why lucy was still talking there has to pull her side and he peaks to the council of lou interrupting the conversation and then apologising while telling her himself that she had just received an award and that they should leave before the council changes their minds.

Lucy tells Benjamin to stop it as it ws their council she looked like she was in control as benjamin finds out that she knows the same as him. And that they were just trying to butter her up. Benjmain tells her again tat they had to leave. If she stays any longer she would get them both court marshalled. Lucy has lost and benjmain just as she wakes up.

Lucy realises who she has been talking to she finally bows down to Benjamin s arguments. As he also apogees and as she finally grabs benjmain taking him out side of the court room. Another conversation begins about Lucy's attitude it ws totally wrong benjmain has to explain to her.

He continued tat she would get them both arrested talking like that. He continued you cannot talk to those people like that Jesus Christ lucy when are you going to wake up your spirit five now get used to it.

Lucy bows down to what benjmain had said benjmain continued if you like being a part of the spirit five team planet let me know come on tell me. Ill make some arrangements lucy looks at benjmain hard as he continues to talk all lucy has to do is say no lucy continued to think while benjmain continued to think he too had over spoken to her an=bout the way he s=feels and the way tat she should feel.

Lucy had finally calmed down and with benjmain and the robot were all back talking positions all the arguing was done and lucy ask if she could take the helm benjmain agrees telling her that the space was hers she could do as she pleases. Ok benjmain you take the helm lucy took what benjmain had siasd as a joke benjmain ws startled by what lucy had done. And he had said only to return to the helm of the space ship a few moments later.
Benjmain was confused and he knew that her attitude was playing a part. Benjmain was feeling nervous for the first time telling her while at her side in the seat next to her that they are heading towards the asteroid field. Lucy jumps waking up benjmain laughs saying the words calmly, as he repeats himself again.

It was what was left of the asteroid field a belt of rocks nothing else. The asteroid field ws not there concern as for the planet tat had been removed to cause it created it tht had been destroyed as another warning to the humans a couple of million s of ,miles away.

Benjamin knew it would be all over the news back on planet earth. Benjamin had time to argue about it was obvious that it was his planet that did what it needed to do just to get the idea to some jumped up scientists that think they know what we are thinking and so on. Just to get the idea across to the leaders of the planet earth. Even so none of them saw any difference it was down to chemical imbalance chemical imbalance my arse of the planets astrosphere I had heard enough. If there ws enough imbalance the planet could cause an explosion. It ws felt by the planet earth however you n=may like to put it. Except this tie it was only Saturn was it to far away from the earth as to give them a warning.

As for the scientists they have very little knowledge of what is really happening out side of three tiny universes. Benjmains computer could understand all of there years and years of knowledge within a minute's and give them the answers benjmain planet lou was that far advanced than the earthlings and the planet that a whole.

As Benjmains computer would have all the facts as it was watching and listening and at this time the computer was sending a message out to te hitman tey had some explaining to do. The computer ws playing a=catch up.
Something happened and it happened fast a few hours ago via the three days before. Three days and three hours was what the computer was trying to say.

The earth lings were ready to except the challenges there messages it came up on the silhouettes computer screen however it ws a lie it was made up the council of lou had lied about the destruction of the earths fellow planet and needed some body to take the blame for a while it settles down in and amongst our people.

Even though the humans brought it and it web know further benjmain was left to continue his job in finding his target lucy too they both get onto the mood and want some action. The robot is perfecting the space ship. To head to the planet earth all three of them not forgetting the sunflowers they could feel the imbalance it was clear that the removal of an actual planet in the earths solar systems was going to have an effect on everything including the planet earths future life in that solar system. On the earths people and the earths systems.

What was done the council could not bring the planet back and it was a warning to the planet earth. The council continued and he thought nothing of it really did not like the human race. Benjmain ws slowly catching on.

It really ahd not sunk into benjmains mind what the council the city of lou on the planet of lou was actually doing. What they had done to the earth atmosphere and the planets nears them. The earth solar systems had been attacked one whole planet destroyed simply for what nothing amongst the planets people who were going to take the blame.

They claimed it was a warning to the people the earthlings on the planet earth. It was the human race.

Meantime the silhouette was showing benjmains some real power, and the earth ws lucky that there ws nobody inhabiting it Saturn the planet no more exists because it ahd just been destroyed. In the near future this would have an effect on the rest of the worlds unseen by man its self ait would effect the earth soar systems continuously there was no knowledge anywhere of any such space disaster nobody knew it was coming.
And that they said was the beauty of it. The silhouette boasted to his council as they did the same. Lucy ws really disappointed leaning over to benjmain as they sat watching and listening as she was lectured about what happens with the solar systems when another planet is destroyed. This hole thing and the subject ahd left benjmains actual work side tracked he still has to find his target and he knows that time is slowly running out. Benjmain says nothing and continued to listen as the summary had just finished lucy again leans towards l=benjmain telling him tat she ws feeling disappointed and the fact that it was why they were there tro stop things like that happening.
It just does not make sense why would anybody want to blow up a harmless planet its crazy. They do not realizes any of them that it was there own council ordered by them and oders were taken by the silhouette.

Once again the council tells its people of this so called great tragsy the removal of the planet in the humans solar systems. They concluded that it was a warning to the earths inhabitants and better things will happen on the earth when realizes its changes. As the council boasts about there reasons benjmain is well unimpressed with his attitude towards other planets it ws a harsh reaction to some thing that had not happened yet benjmain continued to benjmain continued to lucy which was by his side that it ws good that there was rumours that they had visit the planet. However about its destruction lucy and benjmain agreed to close there eyes and with in a few seconds all the stress was gone however only to bump in to the silhouette why was incidentally doing the same. The blame of the planet ws being past about. The earth thought it was them and in other places it ws said it was by scripture and the council said nothing.

There was a battle of mind s arising Benjamin says nothing to start with he did not the many layer sin his eyes the thought suddenly kicks in Benjmains temper arises he is up wards lucy was clever enough to see what was going to happen to see what was bothering benjmain clever enough as she had previously had experienced the same way back I the spirit five. This time it was the silhouette Benjamin had happened it was no longer the suit or badge it was a power of minds as benjmain thinking that it ws him ahd trapped his mind in side of the silhouettes mind . the question ws did the silhouette know and would benjmain be able to find his way out of there.

Benjmain knew that he ws in trouble anyway and ws looking for a way out even before he had get in side of him. As they both land face to face in the jungle benjmais remembers it him self. This ws way back in time at the very beginning benjmain remembers..

As benjmain is being challenged and once being re sured by lucy tat he once again being feeling confident. Once benjmain is sure about his where abouts the silhouettes conversation starts to begin. The silhouette knows that benjmain has trapped himself in his mind benjmain now knows he was put inside of his mind on purpose. The silhouettes conversation begins.

Lucy and Benjmain wake at the same time both rearing to tell each together about the dream they had they had dreamt the same they thought tat it was seriously weird. As benjmain is trying to explain lucy is doing the same. They stop at the same time and stat at the same time. They bump into each other at the same time and appogises at the same time until one of them sits down ahh right no right she says again following Benjamin. Benjmain needs to tell explain to lucy what he had just experienced.
They both agree that they ahd both had the dream of the silhouette. They were both confused thinking that the council was again was about them double cross the team and use the silhouette to find them and destroy them well rty. too. this was quite worrying as the silhouette in the right frame of mind which while under Benjmains knowledge was if it ws the silhouette they would be hunted until they were dead just the name frightens me. Lucy says joking.

Benjmain and lucy have a new talking point the silhouette he was on top of the with benjmain smiling he s food lucy he nearly had me I should of seen that one coming spirit five list at that time and benjmain realizes the time and remember that he also has a job to do. The conversations tat they were having were above there heads both of them.

Benjmain was already getting ready for battle and he knew tat the word ws out there waiting for him the silhouette was prepared he was not waiting around he was coming straight for benjmain it was lucy who had said those words benjmain still was unimpressed benjmain was nice and cool about it. There was anew problem.

Benjmain at that moment was confident that himself and the spirit five team with its super powers built in to gte spirit five badge would be educate in matching the silhouette for his own super powers.

All the talk of the silhouette hunting benjmain down was getting and putting benjmains in a bad mood. One moment he was having a converstion with lucy the next he was in a bad mood then he was asking lucy if they could just go and hide at the bottom of the ocean it would be safer there. Lucy was having to man up as Benjamin was getting nervous.
In a instants lucy knew once they had left ither way benjmain ws defiantly caught up in the silhouettes mind. As benjmain changes his mind thinking that he could deal with the problem later on and having the idea tat he would be better of hiding the fact tat he wanted to fight the silhouette e but felt that he would be able to hurt him first by not turning up for the confrontation he believed that he should take an eye out of the council and turn the other cheek,

Benjmain could see what was happening as so could Lucy who was not to far away as for support. Lucy you did not experience the same as me she answers yes I did the silhouette had tried to enter Lucy's mind through benjmain and then the robots mind. Some people lucy continued they prefer to out rather than in as does benjmain answers her. As the silhouette makes a move gto pull lucy which is what he said he ws going to do in the council rooms.

The talk about the silhouette hunting down benjmain was putting benjmain in a mood one moment asking lucy of himself and her would like to go back to the planet and have the battle. Then understanding after Lucy's answer he would change his mind he was defiantly caught up with some thing in side of his mind. As benjmain changes his mind again not being able to make up his mind to make that simple discussion he goes and lays down after winning his mind back from the silhouette or even more so the creature that dwelled inside of him had freed him the silhouette.
Benjmain could see what had happened as lucy could feel not the same but the mood that benjmain had left himself in. benjmain was smiling and speaking to lucy at the same time telling her that the monster was good. He asks lucy if she ahd experienced the same as me. Lucy agreed that the silhouette had just tired to enter

the spirit fives teams minds. Everybody experienced some kind of interference within the last hour or so.

Some people lucy continued to say that some prefer it in rather than out. Benjmain answers saying to her that she cannot be serious lucy says yeah I would put him inside of it would be hell but think about the people we could save. Benjmain looked at lucy you really mean that do you not.
Lucy replied if it ws possible then yeah. He would be in control of you lucy it's a good idea a dam good idea except I am not willing to lose you yet. Benjmain continued . lucy ecologies benjmain and they both know where they are standing the conversation beings again you mean to put him inside of your mind. Lucy smiles and says to him that she did not say mind. As the mind and the body could be separate as they grow.

Benjmains smiles where does your knowledge come from lucy reply s was by observing
Fully in my mind like hidden inside of me ok how do I put him in me. Well it would start by greeting him in to it io guess. The second would be how do I stop him from destroying me once he his in side of me.
Benjamins answers was a good one he says to lucy that he would fall through her in to her body. From his mind he would only be there from a short time.
It's a good idea but for now I think that it is too dangerous. Lucy shy's away too dangerous benjmain answers again lucy your incredible however I am not going to lose you to that monster, ok decision made go and take your mind of it. Because the answer again is no.

Lucy continues ignoring what benjmain was said and continues the conversation how do I stop him from leaving myself once I have him in me trapped inside of me. Lucy agreed it was a different idea however it was just a solution if they ever needed one it could work if they both would think about it.

Benjmain tells lucy that he needed to lay down and that it would be more than just a dream that would be bothering him at that time. Lucy agrees as usual and Benjamin tells her if she could take control of the space ship. As benjmain closes his eyes and uses his mind to follow and observe the silhouette he was defiantly in side of benjmains head the battle of mind had begun. In benjmain on the spirit five.
It had started when benjmain went to plug himself in for a recharge to re energize his space suit he could feel the power and lucy says she could feel the presents and the silhouette had just blown up on the entire planet. Both lucy and benjmain ws concerned.

Chapter 7

Lucy was the first to break the ice, and basically tells benjmain that it was lucky that nobody had inhabited it. Even though the planets destruction did not cause any harm to the planet earth giving lucy to believe that it was a good sort after plan and it was a warning. The next question was could it of been the silhouette the answer again ws probably how though, benjmain s says what with his mind. Lucy continued its feasible his mind can be just as power full. Th
e only other answer that lucy could find with out using her teams robot and computer was that there must have been some kind of chemical I balance in the solar systems.

Benjmain feeling sad could feel the sadness of what used to be there. He now believed with all the solutions and ideas of how it had happened. Now realizing that it ws true the council did not care and they were lying.

And either way they were happy about being part of the earth destruction it ahd become a game with them.

The silhouette was becoming more powerful and wih the council on the planet of Lou they were slowly dying. The silhoutttee ws calling upon to make there decisions, he would be calle ed to council and make discissions for the planet earth. As the council agree again that they are losing control.
When lucy finds out what's giving the orders she flips and having to break the news to the team. Benjmain was not happy that once again then council had chosen the silhouette over benjmain and his team. Benjmain now too ws losing control he did not hate anybody or pity people the silhouette for trying to be bad and do good at the same time which fitted benjamins profile to a tee.

We all know tht the silhouette was going to come after benjmains team, if anything should happen to benjmain it could change the future of the human race.

Lucy and benjmain knew that they were in trouble, and it was just a matter of time before they would meet in battle again. With the silhouette. Benjmain ws in two frames of mind neither feeling happy or feeling sad. He could feel that he was in danger and decides to return to the space ship and move it from the earth to the earths atmosphere up above ion the ozone layer then feeling that there ws something wrong there decides to send them all the way back down to the earths and further down in to the bottom of the earths oceans.

A place where the silhouette could not find them and it was a place that the silhouette could not enter the seas on earth surrounded it like a second body.
Benjmain ahd lost his passion as for watching the sea life mainly sharks at that time. They would usually come right up to the space ship and them bumping the spirit five ws a real thrill to benjmain and it scared lucy a bit.

Benjamin would turn everything off it seemed so peace full down on the bottom of the sand sea beds. Benjmain needed time to think he knows that the silhouette was watching and waiting for them to return. The battle of minds had begun it was like being on a chess board except the only pieces were himself and the silhouette and this war was defiantly one of the minds.

Benjmain ws being charged except it was not a physical battle it ws a phycological battle a battle of wits and mind and a battle through the minds. The silhouette was powerful and benjmain was hoping that the spirit five team once all together would be as powerful as the silhouette themselves.
As they bring and put there minds together. Another gift via there space suits and badges.

A battle of wits had begun that was the first part of the battle he knew that the silhouette was there already waiting for them. A spiritual battle through there minds had begun, of the spirit five. Lucy makes the first move for benjmain she ws not shy of battle and when it comes to battle she is good. The silhouette was just about to fin out and lucy too was trying to put herself to the test.

As she appears to the silhouette in his mind and gives it a thump just to let him know that she was there the silhouette continued to talk to her as he recites as he recreates himself and is putting himself way back in to and further in to his mind hoping that lucy would follow him. The they would meet. Each other.
A small verbal battle begins and benjmain catches on he had forgotten to tell her that the silhouette had taken a fancy to her. Which explains why he chose her to battle with first.

Until lucy is destroyed and thrown out of his mind ending up back in the spirit five space ship. After what had happened after the experience and the experiment they both agree to find a different way. The battle of telepathy ws now on benjmain agenda however it did not work either at that instance.
Benjmain knows and tells lucy and the robot to prepare themselves it was going to be a one to one and a three way conversation.
Were going up stairs to be some bate, buckle up Benjmains words were spoken as the spirit five leaves the darkness of the pacific ocean to the darkness of outa space.

Benjmain raises the spirit five up out of the ocean the space ship certainly made an appearance its sliver colour and it shape pointed rounded nose benjmain raises it nicely and slowly as then water flowed over its streamline body up out of the ocean as the water falls down wards like a water fall its systems were silent and ready. The only sound was the flow of water fallimng back intio its ocean. The sea the pacific ocean.

Then suddenly but silently its engines kick in and there are on there way the spirit five had awoken and lucy was excited it was a real thrill as for benjmain making the perfect take off was noted down by his partners the robot would only the robot would be complimented by lucy shortly after wards.

A few moments later the spirit five grew are up above the earth in above the ozone unsighted and are sitting watching the earth again. As there ws some human interference with them leaving the earth. Benjmain has to cloak the spirit five. Turn on its shields and close his visors. There would be no watching the planet earth for a day or two.

It looked like the humans were about to travel back to the earth shortly. According to the robot talking to the computer they were nearly ready benjmains computer does not gets things like timing wrong he was precise.

The computer and the robot were talking when the computer interrupts itself saying that it had sighted a

object moving fast around a few thousand miles away it would Reach them within a day of two. The robot asks the computer if it could be more precise the computer give s the robot three more answers. The robot was impressed as the computer gives the robots the answers that it ws looking for.
They both thank each together and part. It ws the silhouette and he was moving fast however it was not in there direction yet which benjmain thinks that it was going in a different direction to trick them he had seen the manoeuvre before he says that's it was an ancient battle move. He had done the move on purpose he tell the robot to keep tracking hi. Through its systems and benjmain was made well a wear and was now watching him closely too.

Benjamin could hear the silhouette he was inviting benjmain and his team back down to earth for another battle, the silhouette ws still himself in space himself and now benjmains gets the idea now of why he was being fooled by the silhouette he was wanting another battle.

Knowing this took a bit of pressure off the team. Still they had not forgotten why they were actually there as they still ahd a target to eliminate. Benjamin checks the time everything ws in order.
Benjmain could hear the silhouette s voice as clear as a the daylight it was liken he ws standing right in front of him. Benjmain concerned asks lucy fi she had heard anything or seen anything they agreed for a minute that they were both thinking a lot and they were moving quite quickly. Was observed by both the robot and the ships computer and as the robot and the computer both

agreed that the object that they ahd seen in the distance was the silhouette.

After a brief discussion and a small conversation they all come to agreement to follow it down to earth slowly as benjmain did not want to get to close however it ws obvious to benjmain tat he was going to have to meet the silhouette.

It looked like they had both chosen the destination of where they were going to meet it ws right in the middle of the Sarah desert in Africa, there was a lot of space and it as the perfect ideal place for a battle in the open knowing that the spirit five team would suffer just about the thought of it. And benjmain remembers the last time he was there.

Benjmains space ship settles hoovering over a reasonably high sand dune, but only a few feet above it. This particular place ha been untouched for many years from humans and aliens,
Meantime benjmain is getting some press as his space ship ahd been spotted.

The robot and the computer bumped straight into some film footage of the spirit five, benjmain knows that if he his plans of leading the silhouette back to the city there ws going gto be a police presents about them to greet his welcoming.

The silhouette luck ws just about to change for the worst the booster s on this space ship had failed the silhouette ws a problem in him self now he had two. Mind you this does not make it any easier for benjmain because now the silhouette just does not want benjmain dead but now wants his space ship as well. As the computer gives the coordinates to the robot and benjmain finds out the creature s where abouts his coordinates it ws in the deserts nothing had changed. Only for the silhouette to have a crash landing and now he ws with out a space ship to save him. The Robot and the computer are busy gently argument as they are trying to figure it all out letting benjmain know that a few things had changed.

When lucy finds out what the robot and the computer were discussing she tells benjmain who ws far from happy as he was preparing himself form battle.

It was like the silhouette was right about standing there with the evil look upon his face it ws one of certain death would bring.
Benjmain knows who's he is in touch with and he ws following him closely as the silhouette ws giving benjmain the instruction of how to find him. With benjmain being in his mind all benjmain had to do is follow him. If the name however ws not enough to understand the silhouette
Newly formed plans he says to himself that first he would attack benjmain mind full punishing him every thought I will take and crush them then I will bring them back to lou where I will make the final battle and bury him, believing so much that he could destroy benjmain and the distraction of the spirit five badge that the silhouette sort after as much as benjmains death.

Benjmain see everything the silhouette had spoken it was a visual experience as he watches them both in battle as benjmain mind receives the images of what was to come. Benjmain saw little more of what ws a hallucination from the stat to the finish benjmain needed to act quickly as he needs to change the future he needed to tell lucy of what he had seen and as he witness his own death lucy is busy playing it cool. Telling Benjamin that there is away of changing it benjmain who ws just coming out of shock regain his breath only to stop breathing again when she tells him it would only work in reverse if he destroys the silhouette until before the battle come to that point. It would only happen if he defeats the silhouette. Benjamin continued I knew you were going to say that robot give me some advice is there another way the answers the same as lucy. Benjmain smiling says well so much of r a second opinions as far as they go.

Benjmain now understands he is in a battle that he cannot get out of. Neither Lucy or the robot could help him. Benjamin ws more than prepared benjmains tells himself that he hopes that the suit and the badge hold out. Lucy ws there to helping him you will feel fine benjmain feels tat he ws not as good as he thought you will do good benjmain bet you kick his ass, good. Lucy commented on the subject in question.
However the compliments did nt change the way that benjmain was thinking. At that time as for the visons and things looking horrible on his side of te things watching himself getting his ass
Was not part of the deal. Once lucy had understood him the real problem was the visons and images she understood benjmain.
Is there no answer benjmain asked lucy and the robot both say no. only if you want a real maniac taking control of what you believe in. then replacing it was another one a false one.

Benjmain kindly reclined and said no lucy and the robot look at each other and just as they were going to approach him on that idea he says no again they both look disappointed and benjmain had a grumpy look on his face a disgruntled look of not k owing where to turn or what to do and even what to think all he could do is to wait for the silhouette to arrive and then make his next move. Unsettled as benjmain was.

Chapter 8

Benjmain is preparing himself form a shuttle ride down go the planet earth lucy says nothing until she is invited. She tells benjmain that she has his side she agreed while speaking to benjmain that the silhouette had the upper hand and he knew that he was a little more power full then the badge or no badge. Benjmain plus the badge, benjmain was confident with his powers a little more than lucy.
And he was confident enough to believe that his powers were as good as the silhouettes lucy just wanted benjmain to be careful benjmaìn ws prepared he ws waiting for lucy to intervene in fact Benjamin was stuck in it deep. It had been sometime tat benjmain had been in a one on one battle he was just realizing exactly what he had voted himself in for and he ws realizing what the council and how serous the council actually was. On the planet of the CITY OF lou Had pressured him in to doing as Benjamin steps out of his space ship controlled by his badge his feet touch down on to the sand. As he kneels down having a fresh battle ground where the dead would not disturb him, yet. As he looks upwards whilst kneeling looking in to the distance as he scopes the entire area looking for any other signs of life. Believing that the silhouette was nearby in the distance waiting for him to revile himself to him. Benjmain was expecting some cannon fodder it was the usual way.

He ws talking to himself saying to himself my fore father may I exist and may I have faith in thjios battle these swords that he spoke were of ancient times ancient words and only spoken by him and the robot knew what kind of prey it was as for the way that he recites it. It was a prayer that benjmain was saying. He finishes with bless the ground I walk upon.

As benjamins travels he knows that he was on good ground. Lucy is close behind him benjmain is unaware that she was following him. She calls out hay benjmain turns around what was the answer to her. Good luck. She says which ws her last comment. She continued that he was not a lone and she would be there close by she had got benjamins back.

Lucy reminds benjmain that they ahd to be somewhere else benjmain looks at the time as he lifts his head up front his watch it was a good excuse for benjmain to start a conversation that benjmain, lucy and silhouette were going to have.

Benjmain knows not to over use his name he had the tendency in turning up.
Benjmain realizing exactly what she was saying there was going to be stand off. lucky for Benjamin lucy has his back. Benjmains says it looked cowardly as for lucy following him. But it made sense.
And seemed correct benjmain had to remind himself that he was there to do a job lucy reminded him benjmain had forgotten. Too kind for the silhouette, alone in the distance waiting for benjmain to rev appear which did not happen as he was needed else where as for that time.

Benjmain bows out as for the confrontation he shouts believing that the silhouette was not there he was being set up meaning that he must get back to the new park city park as the silhouette ahs benjmain business there.

And it ws true that benjmain had business else where referring to following the silhouette back to the city.

Benjamin explains to lucy that he had been set up benjmain was back on the spirit five and heading back to the city as for having to explains why what and when was it going to happen. The computer as well as the robot and lucy all have benjmains back. The target was away from the hotel leaving a small convoy of police cars which would shortly be arriving another sat up from the silhouette. Heading out of town and through the most venerable part of the city and towards another desert benjmain was happy to hear the news he was feeling busy as he ws going gto kill not justv his target but the silhouette also.

He believes and he hopes that he is not impossible to remove the both of them with one attempt. Benjmain was in a mood as the space ship the spirit five was slowly catching up with the convoy with was part of a set up as the silhouette ahd sent them into the wrong direction. As the spirit five slowly catches up with the convoy benjmain finds out that he is not he only person that wants the target dead. It looked like the oxygen and the hitman were part of the deal, as well.

There appearance so late in the programme leaves Benjamin in a state of confusion as he did not understand why they were trying to intervene at such a late state. And he did not know who the new too cops were and the car name. the question was had somebody tipped the cyber police off that's what benjmains thinks as the oxygen and the hitman enter the scene. It also looked like benjmain was going to make the hit that benjmain was supposed to do. By the council on his planet.

It looked like the target was wanted not just by benjmain. And the council of lou now but it looked like the oxygen and the hitman were in on the deal. It was just going to be a matter of time they were all thinking about the hit who was going to make the first move.

Lucy, benjmain and the silhouette were all thinking the same. That they could be killing wo birds with one stone. The silhouette wanted revenge Benjamin and lucy while benjmain and lucy were more interested in the target, as for the silhouette as benjmain puts his target first benjmain and lucy in the sprit five head off to find the target not knowing that they were still being followed by the silhouette who was being followed by the oxygen and the hitman.

Benjmains had lost sight of the target all he knew was that he was in a building some place benjmain has no time to find him and tells himself as he tells lucy while they are talking that discussing it with the robot and the space ships computer and deciding weather or not they should blow up the hole idea.
Benjamin thinks that they do not have a choice lucy half agrees as the changes are set this happened quickly after another good look around the building for the

target and lucy gives him the ok as she has his back. Lucy again tells him the same that she had nothing.

Benjmain sets the timing on the explosives for exactly half an hour. Leaving with the charger with himself if he ws to abort there ws nobody about just the sousnd of silence and then the occasional bird tweeting other than that nothing. Only for benjami to lose sight of lucy forcing him gto stop then clock and stop the disrtuction of the building and the target.

Lucy was in the building no, longer looking for the target. She was now looking for Benjamin as he was standing aside outside gritting his teeth thinking and telling himself that she better hurry up. He could imagine lucy walking around in there casually like nothing was going to happen. Pleading for lucy to come out of the building that was just about to happen. He ws just about to destroy.

Lucy finally makes an appearance benjmain has to question her she claims that she was out side at the back of the hotel and that she knew that he ws going to blow up the building as she had seen the samtex which ws why she was heading in his direction and hailing him to expect her return as benjmain looks downwards at his belt noticing the bule and white flashlight he turns it off. realizing tht he may of given his position away which was what a lucy was trying to say.

Benjmain answers her with an URH. Ok anything else there ws no sign of the target yet. As lucy speaks to benjmain telling him that she had looked everywhere and she ws also unhappy about benjmain setting up the device while she ws still in the building.

As he presses a couple of buttons and within a few seconds the bleeps stop benjmains mind is clear slowly now to think that all the waiting around was bothering him. He had now stopped his mind saying that the target had already been removed.
The pressure was off benjmain the council will praise him when he gets back to his planet however it was not over yet the silhouette was just about to make another appearance however at this point benjmain did not acre and his mind in the right frame was still ready for battle. He was up for the challenges and is ready for a fight.

The silhouette had found benjmain quite easy benjmain made it clear that it ws easy to find him because he wanted to be found by him and so. There was a large stand off nobody wanted to make the first move the silhouette was growling and occasionally grunting as benjmain was playing it cool he was ready and nice and clam still standing bottling it all up. Waiting until he ws upset enough to make the challenge. As benjmain nudges closer to him.

In the end he draws a line across the floor reminding him self that it ws te silhouette that ws infront of him. Benjmain taps his badge he is looking for eye contact and he is beleiveing that the silhoutee had forgotten about him he seemed to be focused on some thing or some body else.

He tapes his badge sending a message back to lucy who was close by and cloaked in side of the spirt five space ship. As the badge asks lucy a few questions with benjmain leading he asks lucy if she could see or hear anything unusual different from the normal as benjmain thinks that the fight was not his but Lucy's. As the silhouette seemed to be watching her. And totally not focused on benjmain.

Benjamin touches his badge explaining to lucy that there target and the silhouette wanted tom battle with her and not him. He continued to lucy was she feeling fit enough to battle them both. Lucy was not a coward and tells him straight as long as he has her back she wanted in.

Out of the darkness the two cyber cops appear and as they do they are talking about the oxygen as he tells benjmain that the silhouette had been watching them and they wanted to know why. As the hitman and the oxygen reintroduce them self.

The silhouette for the first time feels that he was in danger five against one as he smiles that off and at all of them they approach his circle.

It did not take long to for the seven of them to start the battle benjmain was a peace keeper a bringer of peace and with luck by his side and the robot tracking and controlling his every move some times not all the time. As for the silhouette had control over nothing however he makes the first move.

The oxygen and the hitman were well a wear of both the spirit five and the silhouette weapons.
The battle which commences had begun as the silhouette makes the first move wiping out with his a large spear like pole at the oxygen twice and he misses twice looking disappointed as the silhouette try's again and misses again leaving himself this time open for an attack himself. He was expecting and attack back it did not happen this time around.

Benjmain being a peace keeper finds himself right in the middle of both off them only to find himself being attacked as both of them forget about each other and decided unconsciously to attack benjmain as they both miss as benjmain is pulling off some seriously cool move as for avoiding what looked like an attack as he

ducks and swivels around the silhouettes pole and dodges close up gun fire from the oxygens cyber weaponed. As he leaves the oxygen right in front of the silhouette leaving him wide open for the kill. But only manages to injury the cyber cop.
With a mighty roar swings his weapon again at the both of them benjmain once again proving his badge and stepping out in front of the oxygen and uses his shield to block the silhouettes thump with a pole.

Not attentionally as benjmain was there also to keep the peace.

Meantime lucy was dealing with the hitman she ws having a good time at that point they were talking I general until the silhouette large pole like spear hits the ground in front of them both. As the silhouette warns them that they are in battle.
The hitman was going to remove the weapon form the spirit five with lucy being over helpful whilst in battle and a little to friendly the bad good guys tell her not to touch however by tat time the hit man catches on its to late and as he takes on an extremely long electric shock for the spear. It was a reminder of who else would touch it.

The hitman is sizzled with being thrown about up wards about twenty feet. And then another side wards. This made things a little easier for lucy she was left with a little to do she has now got time and the space to battle along side of benjmain as he was trying to protect the silhouette and the oxygen form each As benjmain and lucy meet back to back in battle benjmain is happy to see that she knows what she is doing as the silhouette summons his spear back to him lucy readily greets it his time knowing what its powers was. As she manages to dodge the power of the spear. As the electrical shocks lucy dodges them as the spirit five right the way past both benjmain and lucy and of course the robot. The oxygen and the silhouette hand.

Chapter 9

Then hitman ws just recovering and he looked quite angry lucy was on to him quickly as he unleashes the first attempt of bullets from has weapon at everybody including his partner who was being reminded that he was on there side. The hit reaches for a clip his last one before crashing hard to the floor lucy was also downed to like a American football as she was trying to protect benjmain who incidentally was trying to remove the silhouette. Benjmain shouts to lucy and lucy answers his mind.

We have them lucy and we have time lucy we have them. Benjamin says while in trouble, Benjamin could see reasonable in and sounding like he ws in trouble. Only for lucy to yell about the power that he had remaining ion her suit. Lucy was worried that the power on her suit would run out. She also needed a new charge. Just to comp-plicate things.

The hitman was just re covering and looked quite angry lucy was o to him quite quickly as he unleashes an ray of the first set of bullets from his weaponed again at everybody including his partner who ws busy trying to remind him that he was on his side. The hitman was suffering from shell shock and was discerned in which way his cannon fodder was going. He was out of instinct until he was calmed down.

As the hitman reaches for another clip loading up his weaponed acting crazy and in a hurry he falls to the floor. This gives lucy who invites her self in as lucy is now involved and protecting benjmain who in return is protecting the oxygen who was trying to remove the silhouette.

Benjamin shouts to lucy and lucy answers him his words were we have got the time I have got them benjmains says in trouble again like he kind of noticed only for lucy to yell about some thing about how much power she had left in her suit. As lucy continued to fear that her suit ws going to runout and needed a new charge this would leave benjmain alone for a few minutes. Benjamin looks down on to his wrist its flashing he ws going too to run out of power she needs to make a decision. Play along like nothing was wrong. Or leave the target un guarded for a few minutes that would take to boot up her suit.

Benjmain was in the same position lucy new and could see benjmain punishment benjmain knows that he has to leave the battle ground the question was would the spirit five space ship shields be powerful enough to protect the deadly three while they charge. Once all back in the spirit five and all of them charging up. They discuss there battle plan.

As lucy and benjmain had a greed to back out and go back to the spirit five for a re charge
Benjmain knew that he should of checked the power of the suits before entering the battle.
Before they arrived it ws a stupid mistakes on his account. As benjmain team leaves the oxygen and the hitman to deal with the silhouette on there own. Lucy and benjmain were counting the minutes there only mistakes as well as the oxygens and the hitman was that not only were they charging themselves but they were giving there targets a chance to rest and do the same re - charge.

Lucy and benjmain both bow out, as they both head back to the spirit five both side by side again for a re-charge benjmain knew that he should check the suit systems thinking this time no mistakes on his account. Leaving the hitman and the oxygen to deal with the silhouette by themselves by arms, lucy ws busy counting the seconds which turned in to minutes to re boot them both how ever in the battle three minutes could fell like three years.
It was happening like that benjmain ws first to re charge and lucy ws close she ws a few seconds behind him. As she uncontrolled and unattached the cord form her suit she to now was ready to go in to battle again. Lucy was rioght behind benjmain. Some how lucy gets I there first she is the first to get to the silhouette and lucy gets

a point for courage except with the powers of the silhoutee lucy was looking rather week.

As the silhouette brushes lucy battle moves of peace one side. Lucy could feel her powers and she could feel the silhouette even more as she picks her self up off the floor only to be brushed aside again and once again she picks her self up. Only for this time it was benjmain who steeps in front of her blocking the silhouettes attempt to brush her down on to the floor again only for his attempt to reach benjmain who blocks the whole effort with his shield.

As benjmain manages to knock the silhouettes spear out of his hands leaving him open for a small attack as benjmain trans forms him self in to the tiger and makes a move to wound the silhouette.
As benjmain gets in half way, lucy is on the floor once again she had taken a hit. Benjmain with all the excitement asks her shouting are you ok. Lucy reply was one of anger, there next attack would be a joint effort. however the silhouette had his hands full not only would he be fighting off the oxygen and the hit man he would be fighting off the lucy and the benjmain who had now joined in to the battle.

The silhouette ws kicking ass the hitman and the oxygen were taking the front of it while lucy and benjmain stopping the real damages, they were like a reinforced in this great battle. Which had stated off as there's. This was a great battle in benjmains eyes. This reminds Benjamin as he is watching the hitman take another hit and as he hits the floor he takes another one. While picking himself up he speaks and tells the spirit five team that's another one I owe you.

Only to catch his partner as too who had not been pushed but thrown across the battle ground. As they both get up off the floor as they are raised up by the silhouettes spear like rod as the hit man was just about to speak to the oxygen not to touch the spear he touches it and electrocutes himself the oxygen hits the deck the floor and is out unconsciously. The oxygen is out of the count.

The silhouette believes that he had re moved the oxygen simply by the hitmans reactions lucy ws now content as she had taken a beating lucy could now see the pain that she was in. as for the hitam there feeling over the battle was getting to them all. As the anger of the hitman was over boiling. In all of his anger changes the silhouette who was boasting to himself.
Benjmain could see clearly telling lucy to get to get the hitman's back, lucy does as she ws told benjmain is watching over her the oxygen who a nearly recovered he was recovering slowly never the less he awakes in shock to be coming around by lucy. Who was bring him back around.

Benjmain morphs himself turning himself in to a tiger getting ready to make a second move and hope fully the last as he goes to bite the oxygens head off. only to be attacked form the behind it ws the hitman benjmain sees nothing as he morphs out of himself again becoming invisible as he circles both of them dealing with which one s they should remove first.

Benjmain does not see the silhouette who was right behind him lucy calls to him. The hitman could see him yet he still refuse to yell for him. As benjamins morphs back in to a tiger he is in his most powerful position and in so he finds himself out of the hands of the silhouette and between a fork methodically, benjmain is trapped neither can he morph out of his position Benjamin knowing that the real target ws his badge and he knew that the silhouette could not reach it.

It looked like benjmain ws in a pickled jar, going know where fast as the silhouette has a few words on behalf of himself with out the authority of the council of lou. Not known by benjmain yet who ws giving the orders.

The silhouette roars with anger and then laughter soon after wards stating to all of them that he ws the mightiest power and that he had been waiting for this moment for a very long time.
It was now everybody s turn to save benjmain first the robot and then lucy they both find lucy being the closes to the hitman and the oxygen were pleased with watching benjmain and the position that he was in.

The silhouette was not playing games as he raises his voice with his fork to challenge it was a sword type battle with sword like weapon taking a extremely step back wards and takes a swipe at benjmain who quickly and cleverly disappears only to reappear. Behind the silhouette who indecently turns around only to meet an extremely large tiger. As benjmain leaps up on to him as benjmain is the first to do some damage to the silhouette the silhouette was losing for once. As the hitman and the oxygen who were recovering only to come back out on to the battle ground straight in to another battle. As the robot who was doing all the special battle coordinates as battles are controlled as the robot was ohing and Arhing for most of that battle. As of this round it's the silhouette who gets his revenge as he has the hitman by his bollocks literally while pinning down benjmain on the ground by his throat. Only for lucy to leave the oxygen who is looking like he had been beaten up. Literary again as lucy sees Benjamin only for a second to swap places. As lucy ends up between the silhouette s fork close to the devil but a little closer some how she does it again and lucy remember s not to touch his fork again she could do with out forty thousand volts of the funk. Lucy is clean out and cold she had mistakenly touched the fork but only just.

Benjamin had got free and was on his own with the three the oxygen the hitman and still thee the silhouette. Benjmain knows that he was going to have some explaining to do as he ws in a little bit of trouble. Benjmain has time to think and he was thinking only knowing that it was not impossible to remove all three of them he was thinking hard and He feels the full force of the hitman s weaponed as he blocks it with his space shield reflecting the laser like fodder back to them all and all of them dogging out of the way.

Benjmain as we know has no weapons and he to has to make an approach via his badge he s a tiger again as he clicks his badge as moving fast using his gifts. He s moving fast an changes again once in a more suitable position and distance. As he changes from a tiger only to have been blocked only to trans form and summon up his shield to blocks the drome other cannon fire from the oxygen who was close some how and was not giving up.

Benjmain gets close enough to scratch him and the scratch was not a small one. It was nice and was down his suit the oxygen was not just hurt he ws poisoned too. As benjmain grows at him as the smell of the poison could be smelt through the wind as he grows

again to remind his friends that he too has hidden weapons. Poison claws.
The hitman catches on and he is now moving towards Benjamin as he was just about to bit the oxygens hand off. tht ws the last thing that benjmain had said from that moment.
Lucy was to trying to hide as she ws putting up an extraordinary fight while on top of the silhouette literary hitting him as hard as she could while dodging his fork. Not that anything that she did had any effect on the monster. The silhouette also was looking now like he ahd been taking beating. However, he did not feel again and continued like nothing ahd happened. The silhouette like in many battles he would see what the damage was done at the end.

It looked like lucy judgement and theory s were correct that now as they fight they would only see the damage at the end of the battle especially in the silhouettes case. She had got that one correct. As for her self she ws neither hurt her suit kept her well for battle and she ws enjoying all of the action. Especially the battles. As lucy is thrown off the silhouette back on the floor only to roll and roll of to avoid being stamped on. Only to be saved by benjmain who interdentally was looking a little rough.

He knows the rules he was not to retaliates as like in most combat he would have to be attacked first before his suit would let him make a move, this ws also the case with lucy the suit and badge would only react in self defence.

In anywhere until he is actually touched in aggression it was the same with lucy and the robot they too could only react in self defence.
All three of them were waiting it looked like three on three the hitman ahd just awoken from his shock of touching the fork of the silhouette and he was by the oxygens side and next to him ws the silhouette. The battle continued again. This time it was longer and harder.

This time it was the good old fashioned fight hands and feet no weapons or any funny stuff the fight had moved in to stage sit had become a fight of power super powers no weapons no powers to powers in and at that stage. Everybody had run out al of them needed a break they were not going to get one. Lucy wanted to quite she was knacked out benjmain on the other side of things found himself agreeing as for the sihputte he would left to entertain the two cyber cops the hitman and oxygen.

The attempt to talk to the silhouette did not leave to much of an effect with the silhouette he was not in the business in making friends with earthlings as he called them he ws not up for making any kind of conversations in which he calls earth scum when those two words come out in conversation with the two cyber cops the hitman and the oxygen realize that they were defiantly taking to the wrong person. But the right people.

Within a few minutes they were all ready to battle again it seemed strange that they would all stop to re-charge feeling cooperative and nobody had actually been killed

yet nobody had been left for dead, yet. Benjmain and lucy knew that there was some goodness coming out of three of them. There approach ws one of peace the silhouette neither cared or even thought tat the hitman and the oxygen were trying to their job.
Benjmain is the first opponent was the hitman and as they began Lucy's joins in as benjmain was quick to run into trouble, her words were something of the lines of I've got your back Benjamin the robot and the computer were still there to controlling benjmains moves for a short while about one hundred and twenty moves to be more precise.

The oxygen was too eger to look for battle and ahd bumped straight in to lucy she ws watching not herself but benjmain s back she to needed assistants and calls for it. The robot ws ready to had his job to the spirit fives computer. She ws taking hits just as well and within those few minutes had taken as many hits as benjmain had taken within a few minutes.
Lucy was the target this time around as she is taking hits left right and centre lucy shouts to benjmain who was close as the sound of the gun fire ws making most of the noise it ws quiet battle if there ws one, benjmain shouts back there in control putting the silhouette takes his second hit benjmain is surprised as he had wounded the silhouette for the second time. As the silhouette becomes twice as angry and twice as powerful it ws lucy who he thinks made the wound and not benjmain she to will now have to run, the silhouette now ids fully a where of what damage she ha done it was lucy that had wounded him.

As benjmain boasts to her over what she had done, and continued as they fort that she had conquered the silhouette. Benjmain and lucy switch places as he is having now to protect lucy form the silhouette hand. Benjmains tells her that he has got her back. The fight with the silhouette was now hers. The silhouette would try and deem it as it was now a personal thing however the wound was clean and with the hitman there and the oxygen where soon to realize that it would get the opportunity to attempt the silhouette they could go back in to work in to the silhouette word lucy and benjmain were thinking the same they all were thinking the same.

Benjmain thinks that is good enough the information was good and as for the conversation ends in Benjamin he is all ready making calculations as he sits contemplating his next move everything was going correct and to time.

Benjmain felt within second and lucy felt it also benjmain warns oxygen off him and lucy the oxygen hesitating takes a step backwards off benjmain who disappears he was using invisibility only to trans form. And appear behind the oxygen only to use his stealth to go and find out what was exactly going on. Benjmains gets there to late the silhouettes space ships doors closes tight everybody had stopped to watch the space craft rise upwards off desert sands and manure's upwards in to the sky's.

Once the silhouette day had finished the oxygen and the hitman, lucy and benjmain it all stats over again with a conversation which neither of them wanted.
They were all discussing what the had made the silhouette move asking each other why they had bowed out benjmain a=says that it ws timed he ws not the best of fighters it was his actually powers. It just happened that it ws to just power full for my likening lucy agrees as so does the cyber police whom continue.

As benjmain continued inviting the rest of the battle as he said tat it ws only for him . to kick there asses and continued to temp the hitman and the oxygen whom to were both getting closer to benjmains and lucy. The hitman laughs and Benjamin saw what was coming next too. As he avoids some more cannon fodder.

As an array of bullets follow that the hitman was serious and fires his last bullet in his magazine at lucy unexpected any how lucy ws just as quick as she loads up her shield to protect her it worked as a good defender which she does with Benjamin leaning a cross her also using her shield to defend her from the bullet that was meant for benjmain lucy takes them both one for herself and the other for benjmain both hitting her in different places.

The hitman new that it was definably his move even his partner said it was so.
As for the silhouettes was fool knew when he had enough and he was waiting for the chance to escape the fight and make his run to his space craft.

The hitman too could feel the silhouette fears now as for the oxygen they all speak to each other. They try and speak to each other the hitman catches on benjmain did not notice and that the oxygen ah d disappeared off the scene only for benjmains robot to find a signal he ws close by. The silhouette was closer than they all thought and as of the oxygen he was being kept busy as lucy ws too with ahead on collection of martial arts fighting full on. It ws clear to everybody tat she had the style and her approach ws full on and new it ws a little different as she is pulling all kind s of moves of with the press of a button on her suit. This time around it ws a good old fashioned fight.

Lucy did not even know that her suit could do this and benjmain was just as surprised. Just as benjmain ws about to join in the silhouette returns with his space craft as all the attention turns in his direction as lucy dodges an array of bullets from the hitman as he has his sites on her as well as the silhouette not forgetting that he wants to hold her as prisoner. As the hitman was going to make the move in lucy's abduction it was Lucy's second sense to make a run for it the thought of this action was second to none and she knew that it ws part of her gift as he lines up his weaponed waiting for the silhouette to move.

In to his sight the hitman finally does the job the silhouette takes the first bullet then takes another both ion the same place in the back of his leg was good enough for the cyber cop. Just as he was boarding his space craft.

Benjmain wiyhina second felt it as so did lucy, benjmain warns the oxygen of him again and the oxygen takes a step backwards, benjmain who disappears. He ws using his invisablity only to soon transform back behind the oxygen only to use his stealth to go and find out what was going on. Benjmains is to late the silhouette space craft doors shut. Everybody stops to watch the space craft rise upwards off the deserts sand dunes. And upwards further I to the sky.

Once the silhouette days had come to the end it had finished the oxygen the hitman and lucy with benjmain continue it all starts again with aa conversation which neither any of them wanted.

They were discussing what made the silhouette bow out benjmain said it was timed he was not the greatest of fighters it jut so happened that the fork that he uses is his power nothing more together than that he was as week as us. He looks a little bit powerful but that's his power the power of scare. Lucy agrees.

Who ever took the last shot at the silhouette had missed, and got punished again as lucy ws busy being lucy and did not want to let benjmain or the hitman that she was injured as she stupidly continued. Meantime benjmain was thinking about all of the noise not realizing that a ship in space the spirit five had ben boarded with out anybody's permission, there are rules for this Lucy clearly remember them as she wrote the book of rules.

And the hitman knew this even so he continued. As lucy and the hitman continued to fight in the docking bay. It came to the point that she hit the hitman so hard he fell out of the spaceship. Only to get upon and find himself back in front of the silhouette who was supposed to of been doing a disappearing act some how ws mist on his return and ws back in the battle. His first opponent was the guy standing in front of him. The hitman.
Bad timing I suppose you could of called it. Lucky that the oxygen had the hitmans back. Once again the two cyber cops are together were they were suppose to be. As they battle with the silhouette.

The silhouette was not stupid he ws losing form from the wound that Lucy had left him. He ws looking for another break and this time he will not get himself killed. The wound that he was left was not a small one it ws made worse simply as he continued to take part in battle. The silhouette ws no coward. He was protected by the story's of him. Some people seemed convinced that they were true either way he existed weather or not the story's were true well it was only lucy and benjmais tie to find out. If the so called council of the city of lou and its masters was true.

As for the hitman he was realizing and thinking about who s side he really was on and if it was between both of the alien party's he would chose the spirit five team , observed the silhouette. The battles came to a stand still both and all three of the teams were to tired to continue a was conclude as an draw the game ws over lucy and benjmain were well on there way out up and in to space on there way home. Benjmain knows that he would meet the silhouette again as he prepares this self for another spiritual battle through his mind and a mental one through his mind.

Benjamin already has trouble explaining things how was the question was he going to explain this one and as for lucy the earth being. As she is called by the council. It was just another battle to benjmain he ws getting good, Lucy knew this and ws by his side.

After the epic battle the two cops the hitman and the oxygen , benjmain decide to go and chill down under the ocean he was shark watching for some strange reason benjmain was drawn to them. As benjmain is busy recharging himself his suit loaded together by the suit his body and mind it was good Benjamin thought it had not become a curse yet.
Lucy was thinking the same while sucking back on a drink through straw nice and cold she ws saying. As benjmain ws getting a cheap frill whilst powering up. As he is freed after booting up. His attention turns

towards lucy he starts to question her about her experiences on and after the battle.

And how much she enjoyed it as for being apart of the spirit five crew. As lucy was just about to answer him the robot makes an appearance he too ws ready to ask some questions.

As for benjmain he ws nice and a sleep. With the robot taking control of the space ship lucy slowly falls asleep joining benjmain the robot turns on the shields and puts the visor on and with that puts a tint on the main screen also he sits alone that evening watching the seas movements with the sharks for benjmain some thing to talk about the very next morning.

CHAPTER TWO

CHAPTER THREE

CHAPTER FOUR

CHAPTER FIVE

CHAPTER SIX

CHAPTER SEVEN

CHAPTER EIGHT

CHAPTER NINE

CHAPTER TEN

CHAPTER ELEVEN

CHAPTER TWELVE

www.ingramcontent.com/pod-product-compliance
Lightning Source LLC
LaVergne TN
LVHW041156150826
845673LV00001B/178

9781803021638